I0603822

CYNTHIA HICKEY

KILLER SNAPSHOT

A Hollywood Murder, Book 2

Cynthia Hickey

Copyright © 2018
Written by: Cynthia Hickey
Published by: Winged Publications

This book is a work of fiction. Names, characters, places, and incidents are the product of the author's imagination and are used fictitiously. Any resemblance to actual events, locales, or persons, living or dead, is coincidental.

No part of this book may be copied or distributed without the author's consent.

ISBN-13: 978-1-0881-8655-8

DEDICATION

To God for the endless story ideas, to my husband for his never-ending support, and to all the cozy mystery lovers waiting for the next story.

CHAPTER ONE

I, Kelly Canyon, member of the paparazzi, freelance journalist, author, and actress, snapped a photo of the son of the man who owned most of the land under the movie studios. William Johnson, Jr. paused in the doorway of an abandoned building and straightened his tie. This might seem strange to most people, but most of the acquaintances I knew also knew that Junior was an addict. I chalked his frequenting the building up to meeting his drug buddies.

Since I hadn't landed another acting gig and didn't particularly care if I did, I spent most of my time snapping pictures of celebrities and selling them to tabloids. I made good money and set my own hours. Nothing wrong with that.

I really perked up when Ben Jones, one of the studio janitors, also emerged from the building.

Only he didn't have the swagger Junior did. Ben glanced both ways and scurried off like a mouse with a cat on its tail.

I was tempted to enter the building to see what the attraction was, but after almost being killed a little over six months ago, I erred on the side of caution. Instead, I crossed the street to peer through the dirty, boarded-up window.

Since nothing but a long dark hallway appeared on the other side of the dusty glass, I shrugged and headed to the gym. Not to work out, but to photograph those who did. I was one of the lucky women blessed with a great metabolism.

The wait wasn't long. Brock Hanson, my unofficial celebrity boyfriend, exited the gym and slipped a pair of sunglasses over his amazing eyes. He slung his backpack over his shoulder in one fluid movement. The man was sexy without even trying. He glanced my way and grinned, then strolled toward me.

"Hey, gorgeous." He cupped my cheek and leaned in for a kiss.

I closed my eyes and kissed him back. "Anyone inside I should wait for?"

"The usual, plus that new rising star, Josh Bolton."

"Yummy." I grinned.

"Should I be jealous?" He wiggled his eyebrows, knowing full well no one could top him in the looks department. Add in the fact that he was one of the genuine good guys, and Brock had nothing to worry about.

"Don't be silly." I grinned and snapped Bolton's

photo over Brock's shoulder, right along with a pretty, young woman with a baby bump. "Is he in a serious relationship?"

Brock turned. "I haven't heard. I think he's too new to be part of the Hollywood gossip yet."

My photo would be sure to start the rumors flying. Of course, it could be innocent, and Bolton and the woman just happened to exit at the same time. *Stop it, Kelly. Stop looking for mysteries where none existed.*

"What are your plans for the day?" Brock asked.

I glanced at my watch. "I'm meeting Ruthie and Doug for lunch. She said she has something to tell me. I hope it isn't that they're getting married."

"Why not?" He chuckled. "Would that be so bad?"

"The marriage or the fact it would be to Doug?"

"Either."

I frowned. "It's too soon. My grandmother tends to rush into things. Would you like to join us?"

"Sure. I'll drive and drop you off at your car afterward."

Twenty minutes later, we pulled up to an old-fashioned diner right out of the fifties. The red vinyl booth squeaked as we slid onto our seat across from Ruthie and Doug. A jukebox played an Elvis tune. I immediately fell in love with the place. If the burgers were as good as the atmosphere, I might have found my new favorite place to eat.

We made small talk until we placed our orders, then I fixed my gaze on Ruthie. "What's the news you wanted to tell me?"

Ruthie's eyes sparkled. "After the success of our

premiere last weekend, Doug received a request for a TV drama starring a mother-and-daughter detective team. What do you think?"

I crossed my arms and sat back against the booth. "I'm not sure I want to continue an acting career."

She frowned. "You'll never make the same kind of money taking photos, Kelly."

"I like taking photos, and I'm good at it. I catch people unaware and real."

"You're also good at acting. Very good, in fact," Doug said. He slid a thick stack of papers across the table. "Read the script before making a decision. The part is perfect for you."

"I'll look at it, but no promises." Acting wasn't a horrible way to make money. In fact, after working long hours for weeks on end, an actor got more than enough time off. At the age of twenty-five, it was time to pick a career and stick to my decision.

The waitress brought our burgers and fries in plastic baskets lined with red-and-white-checkered paper. One bite of my bacon, mushroom, swiss burger confirmed the fact this was the best burger place in LA.

Ruthie had remained quiet since telling me of the acting gig, something very unusual for her. After a few nibbles of her club sandwich, she pushed her basket aside and sighed. "They won't take me in the role without you."

I glanced over my Styrofoam cup. "Why didn't you say that at the beginning?"

"I wanted you to want to join me, not feel as if

you have to."

Brock nudged my leg, clearly encouraging me to say something that would make the shimmer of tears disappear from her eyes. My grandmother desperately wanted to renew her acting career. The movie we'd done together was only the beginning. This drama might be the very thing to cement her dream.

"Let's head to the studio," Brock suggested. "Maybe the surroundings will help you make your decision."

I hadn't been back to the studio for a while. Being chased through a jungle set by a mad woman will do that to you. But I nodded. "I've made my decision. If it means that much to Ruthie, I'll take the part." And use the time on the lot to overcome my unreasonable fear of a killer lurking around every trailer.

As if sensing my thoughts, Brock reached under the table and gave my hand a reassuring squeeze. "I'll stay with you," he whispered, leaning close. His breath tickled the fine hairs at the nape of my neck.

Brock dropped me off at my car with promises to meet me at the lot. I drove home and picked up Shutterbug, my rapidly growing German shepherd, and drove to meet him. I'd gotten so accustomed to having my furry friend next to me, I took her wherever I could. I hoped the studio lot would welcome her. Some people had an entourage to protect them, I had a dog.

Shutterbug whined when she spotted Brock leaning against his car in the parking lot. I barely got the car door open before she bounded out and raced toward him.

Laughing, Brock put his hands on both sides of the dog's head and ruffled her fur. "I'm glad to see you too, girl." He glanced up and met my gaze. "Ready?"

"As ready as I can be." I held out a shaking hand to him.

He took it in his strong one. "There's no one lurking here who wants to hurt you."

I hoped not. It wasn't that I was a coward. I'd done what needed doing when Amber Jacobson had chased me and my nemesis, Susan Gilroy, through a plastic jungle. And I just had no desire to repeat the experience.

As we stepped through the gates and I spotted the trailer I shared with Ruthie, I stopped. "Who replaced Amber as makeup artist?"

Brock shrugged. "I haven't met her, but I'm sure she's nice."

"Yeah, Amber seemed nice too, and she turned out to be a killer." I headed for the large building opposite us. The cafeteria seemed a safe enough place to make my reappearance. I could do with a cup of coffee.

Mary, one of the women who cleaned the trailers, spied me from the counter. "You're back."

"Yes, it appears so."

"We've missed you." Her gaze flicked to Shutterbug. Instead of telling me the dog couldn't come in, she turned to leave. "Catch you later." She flashed a smile and headed through a side door.

I stayed where I was and let Brock fetch our

drinks. I figured remaining by the door would not only allow a quick getaway if I got spooked, but I could also slip out if Shutterbug's presence bothered anyone.

With coffees in hand, mine a mocha flavor with a side cup of whipped cream, we headed to the outside eating area. I set the cream on the ground for Shutterbug and took a sip of my drink. With the temperature hovering around seventy-six degrees, I was surprised to see the place almost empty. Rod Looper, one of the janitors, swept garbage near the wrought-iron fence encircling the area. A few actors and actresses read scripts or quietly conversed, but over half of the tables were empty. I shrugged and pulled the script from my bag, intending to look it over while I enjoyed my drink. Setting it on the table, I used a napkin dispenser to keep it from blowing away.

Marilyn Clark, an actress, who had almost been one of Amber's victims, frowned at Shutterbug. Then glancing up at me and Brock, she smiled before returning to reading the papers in her hand. Since Brock had saved her life a few months ago, a smile was the least she could do.

Shutterbug finished her cream and started investigating the area. Of course, her nose led her straight to the nearby dumpster. She gave three sharp barks and looked at me.

I patted my leg. "Come here, girl. There's nothing for you over there."

She barked again and tugged on something. As long as it kept her occupied, I let her be. A few minutes later, she trotted back to me, a brown workman's boot in her mouth.

My blood chilled as I reached for it, then stared into Brock's face. As one, we darted for the dumpster, skidding to a halt at the sight of a pair of men's legs sticking from underneath the trash receptacle.

Brock dropped to his knees and peered under. "It's Ben Jones."

"What?" Rod whirled from where he was sweeping under the tables. "Ben?"

Before we could tell the man not to touch the body, he grabbed the ankles of his friend and pulled Ben into the open.

Ben's eyes stared unseeing at the sky. Wrapped around his throat was a strand of electrical wire. Beside him lay an overturned toolbox, its contents scattered.

CHAPTER TWO

It took a few seconds, but I swallowed back my fear and adopted my father's detective persona. "I really hope this isn't going to become a habit around here." I grabbed a tight hold of Shutterbug's collar.

My legs trembled. I wanted nothing more than to collapse into the nearest chair. Instead, I fished out my cell phone and called the police.

"Detective Lawrence."

"This is Kelly Canyon. I…uh…we, found a dead body behind the dumpster on Studio lot 11. By the cafeteria."

Her sigh rattled the air waves. "We'll be there in ten minutes. Don't touch anything." She hung up.

I turned back to our table. "Where's my script?" I narrowed my eyes and glanced around the area.

Marilyn waved the stack of papers. "I'm just curious. Seems like a great show. I wish they'd cast me as the daughter."

"You're too old." I snatched the papers out of

her hand. "Ruthie may be old enough to be your mother, but she doesn't look it. Especially with stage makeup."

"Shut up, Kelly." Marilyn bolted to her feet. "I'm not even forty yet." She tossed her chestnut-colored hair over her shoulder. "I look good."

"Ladies." Brock stepped to my side and motioned his head to where Detective Lawrence and Sawyer approached. "Save it for another time."

Clutching the script to my chest, I sat in the chair Marilyn had vacated. Had seeing another dead body rattled me so much that I forgot my manners? Shutterbug laid her head in my lap and peered up at me with wise eyes. I smiled and scratched her behind the ear.

With a huff, Marilyn sat in the empty chair across from me. "You're a walking disaster."

I glared her way before glancing at Lawrence's face. She did not look happy.

Shutterbug pulled away from me and growled, putting herself between me and Detective Sawyer. "I'm sorry. This isn't like her at all."

"I'll take a look at the body," Sawyer said, making a hasty exit.

With him away, Shutterbug sat at my feet and wagged her tail as Lawrence patted her head. "Good girl. All right, Canyon, tell me what you've gotten yourself into now."

"Nothing. I came to look at a script and drink coffee. Shutterbug found the body. It's one of the janitors here."

She cut a quick glance to where Sawyer squatted next to the body. "Who's the distraught man crying next to the fence?"

"The other janitor, Rod Looper. Both of them were a big help in answering my questions regarding Lauren Mayfield's murder."

"I doubt they'll be much use this time." She ordered a uniformed officer to make sure no one left, then joined her partner next to Ben.

Brock moved behind me and massaged my shoulders. From the slight tremor in his hands, he seemed to be as rattled as I was.

Two hours later, the few people on the scene were allowed to leave. I couldn't reach my car fast enough. I gave Brock a quick kiss and opened the door for Shutterbug. Her gaze was glued to something behind me.

I turned to see Detective Sawyer standing at the gate. From his pale complexion, I could tell the man was terrified of dogs.

Lawrence shook her head and moved past him. "Chin up, buttercup. It's just a dog." She reached for the handle of her car.

"Wait." I snapped my fingers for Shutterbug to climb in the car, then closed the door. I pulled my camera from my bag and scrolled to the one I'd taken of Ben that morning. "I don't know if this means anything, but I took this a few hours ago." I tilted the camera, so she could see.

She studied the picture of Ben, then scrolled to the one of Junior Johnson. She pursed her lips when she moved back to the one of Ben. "He looks scared. Isn't that a drug house?"

I nodded. "The ME will check for narcotics, right?"

"Yes, but the cord around the victim's neck suggests he didn't die from drugs. Email me those pictures." She slid into the driver's seat of her car. By now, Sawyer had taken his seat in the passenger side. His gaze stayed locked on Shutterbug through the window of my Mustang.

"She won't hurt you, Detective." Unless I told her to, anyway.

"Tell the dog that." He fastened his seatbelt.

I grinned. "I will." I headed back to my car and drove home, pleased to see Brock's car in the driveway.

He sat on the porch steps, rising as I approached. "I thought you might like company after seeing Ben."

"You thought right. Come inside and I'll fix something to eat. Is Ruthie here?"

"No. We're alone." He wiggled his eyebrows.

"Behave." I giggled, still amazed at how he could make me feel like a teenager.

I whipped up my father's famous spaghetti sauce while Brock chopped the makings of a salad. We worked in companionable silence with soft music playing in the background. I turned slowly to watch him toss bits of carrots into the air for Shutterbug to catch.

The man was beautiful. His hair fell over his eyes, begging for my fingers to run through the thickness. His deep laugh sent my stomach into flips. I was falling very hard. But, I'd been burned before and swore never to be the first to mention feelings.

"What?" He glanced up and smiled the crooked

smile that made women swoon.

"I didn't know dogs liked carrots."

"Vegetables are good for them. Apples, too." He tilted his head. "Still shook up? You look flushed. Why don't you sit down and I'll finish?"

I shook my head. "I need to stay busy."

Ruthie came through the front door. "I'm home!"

Shutterbug bounded to greet her.

Ruthie yelped. "Down, girl. Why am I the only person you jump on?"

I laughed. "She likes you."

"A little less liking would be nice." She headed for the wine cooler installed in a lower cupboard and pulled out a bottle of red. "What a day."

"I bet we can top yours." I broke angel hair pasta in half and dropped it into a vat of boiling water.

"Do tell." Ruthie poured herself a glass of wine, sat in one of the kitchen chairs, and toed off her heels. "Hello, Brock."

"Good afternoon."

I took a deep breath and faced my grandmother. "We found Ben Jones strangled behind a dumpster at the studio."

Her eyes widened. "The janitor?"

"Yes."

"Who would want to kill such a nice guy?"

I shrugged. "I don't know, and I'm not going to try and find out."

"Your book releases next month. Don't you want fodder for a new one?"

"I'll be too busy with the television show." Not

to mention I'd had enough danger to last me a lifetime. The book about murdered actress, Lauren Mayfield, promised to be a bestseller. Funny how I wasn't tempted in the least to write another one. Unless…no, it wouldn't be fair to pay someone else to investigate and give me the glory. "Being chased by Amber was too traumatic."

"I imagine it was." She peered at me over the rim of her glass.

"What?" I crossed my arms.

"I thought you took more after your father."

"Not fair. Dad wouldn't want me chasing down killers without the proper training." I glared at Brock. "Say something in my defense."

He scooped the chopped vegetables into a large wooden bowl. "I agree with Kelly."

"Good." Ruthie grinned. "I was just making sure you were over thrill-seeking."

I blinked a few times before realizing I'd been played. "You're an evil woman."

"I know." She toasted me with her glass.

After dinner, Brock and I did the dishes, then joined Ruthie at the kitchen table for a rousing game of Cardinal train, or Mexican train, depending on which part of the country you were from.

Brock held up a sparkly blue plastic train the size of a thimble. "What's this for?"

"To mark your dominoes when you can't play," Ruthie said.

"Okay." He clearly didn't understand.

"Let's play a practice round," I suggested.

"Is this an old people game?" Brock frowned at the boneyard of dominoes. "I seem to remember playing this with my grandmother when I was a kid."

"This is a little different," Ruthie said, frowning. "If it was an old person game, do you think I'd be playing it?"

Just turning sixty, my grandmother refused to acknowledge her advancing age or be called grandmother. I hope old age didn't catch up to her for a very long time. "You might enjoy playing, Brock." I smiled. "Pick seven dominoes." I slapped his hand as he turned one over. "Without looking at them. Then line them up in that slotted tray in front of you."

He groaned and counted out seven tiles, taking the one he'd looked at.

After three hands we were laughing, complaining, and good-naturedly trying to block each other's plays. After nine rounds, I held my arms straight over my head. "I won!"

Ruthie's brows lowered. "I'm sure you found a way to cheat."

"I did not. You're just a poor—"

The window behind me shattered. Something struck me in the back and propelled me forward. I held out my hands to catch myself and scattered tiles off the table and onto the floor.

"Kelly." Brock rushed to my side.

Ruthie screamed.

Shutterbug set off a frenzied round of barking, shrill enough to shatter the window if it didn't already lay in shards around our feet.

"Are you all right?" Brock ran his hands up and down my arms and back.

While I enjoyed his touch, I shrugged loose. "What hit me?"

He bent over. "A rock with a piece of paper wrapped around it." He held up the projectile, a rock the size of his fist. "You might want to get checked out, Kelly. It hit you hard."

"If that would have hit you in the head," Ruthie said, eyes wide. "You'd be dead."

"Maybe." I rolled my shoulders wincing. I could feel the bruise already forming. "What's the note say?"

Brock unwrapped it. "Don't get involved."

"Great. Good advice. See why I said no more crime solving? Someone call Lawrence. I'm—" My head fell forward onto the table.

Brock picked me up and carried me to the sofa. "Stay there. I'm calling an ambulance." He held up his hand. Blood smeared his palm. "Your back is cut."

Ruthie stared down at me. "The detectives are on their way. I'm buying us both a gun and pepper spray first thing tomorrow."

"Why? Neither one of them would have done any good in this situation." Resting my arm across my eyes, I had a sinking feeling I would be drawn into Ben's murder somehow. If things became personal, if my loved ones were in danger, I'd feel compelled to help the police.

"No," Brock said. "I can see the wheels turning in your head. Last time you stayed away until someone painted a skull and crossbones on your porch."

I held up a finger. "Don't forget I was asked to

help because of my proximity to the actors and because you asked me to clear your name."

He took my hand in his. "I know I don't have any right to request anything, but I'd like you to stay out of this."

"At this point, I intend to."

The doorbell rang. Ruthie opened it to the stern faces of Detective Lawrence and Detective Sawyer.

Lawrence approached the sofa. "You hurt?"

"A little."

"Do not interfere in my investigation or I will arrest you."

My mouth fell open. "I have no plans of interfering. All I was doing was playing a game at the table when the rock hit me in the back. Which hurts very much, thank you."

She glanced at Brock. "Did you call an ambulance?"

"I did." He held out the rock and the note.

The detective held out a paper sack for him to drop the items in. "I'll send a squad car up and down the street a few times a day for the next week. Whoever did this will give up and go away if Kelly holds to her promise."

I didn't recall promising anything.

CHAPTER THREE

The ER doctor said I had a bruised shoulder. I could have figured that out for myself and saved the money.

After a restless night's sleep, I sat in bed propped up on pillows and tried to concentrate on reading the script for the first episode of *The Cooper Women*. The show promised to be both exciting and dramatic, making me glad I'd agreed to the part.

My hands fell to my sides. I couldn't concentrate, nor could I lie in bed all day, sore back or not.

I swung my legs over the side of the bed, moving as slow as possible, then shuffled to take a hot shower before hitting the pavement to catch glimpses of celebrities. I couldn't help but wish they'd misbehave. The price went up with naughty photos. I might have gotten fired from the *Hollywood Tribune* after being a murder suspect, but the editor was more than happy to purchase photos from me. So was the *Hollywood Gazette*.

Ruthie asked me once why I drove myself so hard to make a few bucks. Dad had been the same way, having it drilled into him by his father that a hefty bank account guaranteed a secure future. I agreed and did everything possible to achieve that security. I remembered the tough times when Dad was a struggling actor.

Smiling, I stepped under the hot spray of water and let the heat ease the ache in my shoulder. After ten minutes, I shut off the water and stepped out, having decided to wander around the airport in hopes of catching a star entering or exiting. Hopefully, the strange people who frequented LAX would take my mind off the sight of Ben's lifeless eyes.

I patted Shutterbug on the head on my way to the closet that was as big as most people's bedrooms. Ruthie insisted on purchasing Lauren Mayfield's mansion the minute it went on the market, and the two of us rattled around in it like pennies in a dryer. I had no idea why she wanted such a large house.

"You have to stay here this time, sweetie," I told my dog. "Unless you're a service dog, you aren't allowed at the airport." Service dog? Could I? I quickly dressed, loaded Shutterbug into my car, and made a beeline for my general practitioner. After yesterday's trauma, I felt safer with my dog next to me. That qualified, right?

Forty-five minutes later, after a stern talking-to about anxiety from my doctor, I procured a special tag for Shutterbug and we headed for LAX. I felt better knowing she would be by my side and vowed right then and there to never go anywhere without her. Even to the studio to film. She'd taken obedience classes. She knew when to stay when I told her to. I had every confidence she'd behave.

I parked in the parking garage, and with a firm grip on Shutterbug's leash—she was only eight-months-old after all—we made our way to the arrival gate. I found a pole to lean against, made sure my camera settings were good, and told Shutterbug to sit. She complied with a lick to my hand.

Sweet. I snapped a photo of a mega star without makeup as she hailed a taxi. I might not have recognized her if a porter hadn't called her by name. By the time the poor woman slid into the cab, a crowd of eager fans surrounded her. I loved the anonymity of being behind the camera.

The whir of a camera sounded to my right. I turned and faced Susan Gilroy, my nemesis. "Go away. You're going to attract attention."

"No can do. You're an up-and-coming star." She pressed the shutter button again.

I narrowed my eyes. "I should have let Amber kill you." I reached for her camera as the flash blinded me.

"I'm going to title this one, 'New Star Hates Paparazzi and Hides from her Fans.'" She grinned, then shouted, "Hey, look, it's Kelly Canyon." She pointed at me when a group of tourists glanced our way. "Have fun."

"Gee, thanks." I pasted on a grin and greeted the

autograph seekers. Shutterbug sat like a champ next to me. "You should be fiercer," I told Shutterbug, then pulled a pen from my bag and started signing.

It turned out that more of the crowd knew me from my book about a Hollywood murder rather than the one movie I'd done. When I'd finished, I looped Shutterbug's leash around my wrist and moved closer to the airport doors.

Shutterbug strained against the leash and barked as Detective Sawyer exited the building with Junior Johnson. The two seemed to be in a deep conversation until my dog interrupted.

"Control that animal," Junior said, "or I'm calling security."

"She's on a leash. We aren't breaking any laws." I snapped their picture and smiled.

"I didn't give you my permission to take a photo." Junior reached for the camera.

Shutterbug increased her barking as I stepped back. "I don't need your permission."

Detective Sawyer moved to the opposite side of Junior. "Let's go."

"Can't you arrest her for harassment?"

"No, I cannot." He nodded at me. "Have a good day, Miss Canyon." The man couldn't cross the street fast enough.

A horn blared as Sawyer stepped in front of a car, forcing the driver to slam on the brakes. The driver raised his fist, then quickly lowered it when he flashed his badge.

I watched them leave, then turned in time to catch a picture of aging actress, Iris Beacon, struggle with five large suitcases. She had three of them lined up in front of her, each hand clutching the handle of the other two. She moved slowly forward, rolling them toward a waiting taxi.

I clapped my hands and pointed at a couple of porters who would rather talk than help an old woman. Leaving Shutterbug sitting, I rushed forward and hoisted a suitcase onto a trolley before the two lazy porters reached the cab.

"Do not give them a tip, Ms. Beacon. They haven't earned one."

"Shall I give you one?" Her dark eyes twinkled. "You're a dear for coming to help me. Everyone inside was too busy."

"Of course, you don't have to tip me." Mercy, her bags were heavy. Lifting them pulled at my bruised muscle. "Where did you arrive from?"

"Venice. Oh, what a beautiful city." She stood back and posed. "Take my picture for those papers you work for. Fans seem fascinated by the lifestyle of the rich and famous. Make sure you let them know where I've been."

I obliged, more than happy to let the porters handle the rest of her bags. "I hope to go myself someday."

"Keep acting and writing and someday you will. Mark my words." She patted my arm. "I was happy to get off that plane, I gotta to tell you. Oh, the turbulence. Why, I had to take a break in the airport lounge." She leaned closer. "That Junior Johnson is quite a trip. You could hear him over the television."

"Oh?"

"A few too many drinks and he started bragging

to some other man about a get-rich-quick scheme. Doesn't his father give him enough money?" She waved a hand in my direction. "Don't pay any attention to an old woman. I don't get to talk to people very much." She planted a kiss on my cheek, wiped away the lipstick smear she left, and slid into the backseat of the taxi.

I made a vow right then and there to pay her a visit a few times a month. No one should spend their life alone.

A half hour passed, and I grew bored. Time to head to the studio and sign the contract for the television drama.

Despite having Shutterbug next to me, my legs trembled as I passed the outside eating area and made my way to Doug's office. I kept my eyes averted from the dumpster and held onto the dog leash as if my life depended on it. A person would think that six months was plenty of time to get over having to play hide-and-go-seek with a killer, right? The pain in my back reminded me that sometimes life threw things at you that you never suspected.

I opened the door and darted inside, coming to a sudden stop at the sight of Ruthie and Doug kissing. Eew. "I'm here to sign the contract," I managed to say.

"Don't look so shocked, dear. Even people our age like to snuggle." Ruthie caressed Doug's cheek, then moved to a sofa against the far wall.

"I'm glad to see you didn't change your mind overnight." Doug slid a folder across the table. "We could have done this online, though."

"I need to get over my fear of coming here." I

signed where needed and handed the contract back to him.

"I think you need to see a counselor," Ruthie said.

"I have Shutterbug. She is now a service dog and can go everywhere with me."

"Oh, goody." Ruthie frowned. While she now tolerated my dog, she still wasn't a fan of large breeds.

Doug crossed his arms and speared me with a sharp look. "I have to agree with Ruthie. You'll be coming here on a pretty daily basis for a while. You can't be afraid."

"I won't with Shutterbug or Brock with me. It's just going to take some time."

"Louie is directing this series. You know he doesn't take any funny stuff."

"Trauma isn't funny, sweetie," Ruthie said, studying her nails. "I can imagine that being chased through a plastic jungle by a crazy person would have a lasting effect on a person. I'm here to help, Kelly."

"Thank you, grandma, uh, Ruthie." I grinned. "I'll be fine. I promise. It took a year to get over Dad's murder, and I wasn't part of it."

Doug didn't look convinced. "Be at your trailer for makeup at six a.m. You'll receive $50,000 an episode for a total of twelve episodes. Keep it up, and you'll be wealthier than you ever thought. I've also been asked to have you stop acting like paparazzi. You're on this side of the camera now."

"What if I don't want to?"

He folded his hands on top of his desk. "You're

a newbie in the biz, Kelly. Abide by the rules."

I thought for a second. I really, really liked taking photographs. "Can I take them if the actor agrees? Or if I don't take them for the purpose of selling?"

"That would be better, yes."

I twisted my lips. "Fine." I spun and rushed from the office. This was horrible. Doug was an awful man. He'd waited until I'd signed the contract before telling me I couldn't indulge in my favorite pastime. One that brought me in a good deal of cash. Of course, while filming, I didn't need to rely on photographs to pay my bills.

"Well, girl," I said, placing a hand on Shutterbug's head. "Life sure has changed since six months ago. I liked my job at the *Hollywood Tribune* despite the annoyance of some celebrities at getting their picture taken. Now, that's been taken away from me."

Shutterbug fixed her dark eyes on me.

"You're right. I can indulge my love of taking pictures by offering to photograph the pets of celebrities. Shutterbug, you're a genius." Of course, this wouldn't get me any closer to fulfilling my dream of becoming an investigative reporter.

I leaned against my car. The best way to do that was to investigate a crime as I'd done with Lauren's murder. Could I do it again? Could I shove aside my fear and try to solve Ben's death? Write a series of Hollywood murders? Ben wasn't famous like Lauren, but readers would most likely buy a book about the death of a janitor on one of Hollywood's biggest studio lots. A few cases and books under my belt, and I could get any journalist job in the country.

CHAPTER FOUR

Neither Ruthie or myself was excited about a six a.m. makeup. Still, we shuffled our way to our trailer. Ruthie sat in the chair while I sprawled on the sofa with Shutterbug at my feet.

"I don't know why we can't have our own artists." Ruthie closed her eyes and laid her head back. "I'm not exactly a newbie to the Hollywood scene."

"Maybe they're trying to cut costs." I shrugged. It really didn't matter to me one way or the other. I hated the thick makeup, and I didn't care who applied the stuff.

"Good morning!" An overly chipper, frizzy red-haired, freckle-faced beanpole of a woman sang and danced her way into the trailer and set a cooler and laptop bag on the counter. "I'm Lisa Rogers, your makeup artist, and yes, before you ask, Olivia Rogers is my aunt."

Ruthie shrieked and stiffened.

I froze halfway to a sitting position. Please, God, don't let her be another makeup artist with aspirations of acting. That hadn't bode well for us the last time.

Shutterbug approached the morning person, licked her hand, and wagged her tail. I liked the woman immediately. If my guard dog thought she was all right, then so did I.

"Good morning," I mumbled and dropped back down on the sofa.

"Oh, we aren't morning people, are we?" She opened a cabinet above Ruthie's head and pulled out supplies. "Good thing all you have to do is sit there and be still. I want to assure both of you that I am not a murderer. I do not covet anyone else's love. I do not aspire to be an actress." She winked at me.

"You read my book. It hasn't released yet."

"I got my hands on an advanced reader's copy and loved it." She fastened a plastic bib around Ruthie's neck. "When the studio hired me, I was warned not to try to kill anyone." Her smile faded. "Just so you know, I didn't kill the janitor."

"I do hope you aren't protesting too much," Ruthie said, her words muffled under a rag placed over her face.

"Oh, Shakespeare. Love it!"

If Miss Morning Person didn't tone it down a bit, I might change my opinion about liking her. Seriously, so much chattering that early in the morning must be against a law.

"I almost forgot." She opened the cooler. "I hope you like frosty mocha coffee drinks because I brought us all one." She handed me mine and I was back to liking her. "I was told you don't go anywhere without your dog, so here's a cup of peanut butter cream." She sat a Styrofoam cup in front of Shutterbug. "There. Now we can get to work." And just like that she went from talkative to silent makeup machine.

Ruthie and I strolled onto the set at five minutes after eight both wearing dark-haired wigs and navy suits. Tears sprang to Ruthie's eyes as she glanced my way. "You look so much like your father now."

"That is the best compliment." I airbrushed her cheek with my lips.

"You're late." Louie glared from his director's chair.

"Only five minutes, you old grouch," Ruthie said with a grin.

My eyes widened as Louie laughed. What had happened to change him into such a softie around my grandmother? "Who are you?"

"Be quiet and get ready for the scene."

Okey doke, it was only Ruthie he liked. I took my place behind a metal desk in a fake police station and got ready to act.

By noon we were finished and back at the trailer to clean off the makeup and dress back into our street clothes. I watched Lisa closely when Brock stopped by to visit. Other than being her friendly, overly-cheerful self, she really didn't seem interested in taking my man. Or jealous that he was mine.

Brock plopped onto the sofa next to Ruthie while Lisa removed my makeup. "This latest film is killing me. I need to spend more time at the gym if I'm going to be convincing as a kick-butt hero."

I laughed. "You'll be plenty convincing. You live the part. Remember how easily you scaled the cliff to rescue Marilyn?"

"You were right there with me, if I recall." His eyes twinkled.

"Maybe the two of you will star in a movie together sometime," Ruthie said. "Wouldn't that be wonderful? Then you could kiss all the time if you mess up on purpose." She laughed. "That would be such fun. Too bad Dougie isn't star material."

"That's mean." I shot her a sharp glance.

"No, I love the fact that he is ordinary. He's my special cuddle bear." She traded places with me in the makeup chair. "It's a blessing not to worry about some woman trying to steal him. With Brock, you'll always have that worry."

"Hey!" Brock frowned. "Never."

"Because you're a very nice man with good morals doesn't mean that women won't try." She wagged a finger at him. "They will try a lot."

"Can we change the subject, please?" I slid closer to Brock's side. "Life is too short to be jealous."

He grinned down at me. "Yes, it is." He gave me a quick kiss. "What's the plan for the rest of the day?"

"Let's go to the beach."

"Excellent."

By four we arrived at Huntington Beach, loaded down with towels, foldable chairs, an ice chest, a frisbee, and takeout Chinese for supper. We set up our chairs and stripped down to our bathing suits. Shutterbug darted for the water sending a flock of sea gulls scattering.

I laughed. "This has to be my favorite place on earth."

"That's because you've never been to Maui," Brock said.

"How do you know that?"

He laughed and threw the frisbee for the dog to catch. "Because if you had, you would say that was your favorite place."

I shrugged. He was probably right. "I'm going to walk the shoreline before we eat."

"I'll play with Shutterbug for a while, then catch up with you."

I stopped about a hundred yards away. Detective Sawyer and Junior Johnson, both wearing suits but carrying their shoes as they moved barefoot across the sand, headed for a small dune above the wave line.

They seemed like a strange pair to be friends. I shrugged and continued my walk, pretending I hadn't seen them. While I had no idea how to investigate Ben's murder, I didn't want anyone to know I was contemplating the idea.

It had been easier with Lauren. I'd been a suspect, along with Brock. We'd teamed up to clear our names. I had absolutely no reason to get involved this time other than wanting to write another book to further my career.

I plopped down onto the sand. What a selfish reason. I folded my arms around my bent knees. I ought to seek justice for the death of a nice man without any gain for myself. But, wanting to write a book might be the best way to get people to talk to me. Everyone wanted a piece of fame, even if only in the acknowledgments of a novel.

Shutterbug barreled into me, knocking me onto the sand. I laughed and wrapped my arms around her neck, dragging her down with me. "You always know just when I need you."

Brock sat down next to me. "You looked deep in thought. Do you need to talk?"

I sighed and met his gaze. "You won't like it."

"Maybe not, but I'll still listen." His mouth quirked.

Taking a deep breath, I blurted, "I've decided to investigate Ben's death and write another book."

He exhaled slowly and stared at the ocean. "Have you told your grandmother?"

"Not yet." After a while of considering the idea, I felt pretty certain she'd want to join me. My grandmother craved excitement.

He leaned back on his hands. "I guess I'll have to be your bodyguard again. I'm sorry I didn't do a better job last time."

"You broke your leg saving Marilyn's life."

He shrugged. "I should have done more to prevent you from almost being killed."

I put a hand on his shoulder. "Stop. If you want to join me in this adventure, fine, but you are not responsible for any trouble I may get myself into."

"You know I can't sit back and let you walk into danger without saying something." His gaze warmed. "What happened to your fear?"

"I've chosen to shove it down out of sight, never

to be seen again.”

“That sounds healthy.”

“Don’t lecture.” I stared back at the lapping waves, then pushed to my feet. “I’m hungry. Ready to eat?”

He chuckled. “I’m always ready to eat. Someday, I’m going to stop playing the heartthrob hero roles and eat whatever I want whenever I want.” He took my hand in his.

We strolled along the water’s edge, leaving Shutterbug to chase birds and follow at her own pace. “Ruthie’s never had the freedom to do that. Women can’t get a paunch and still get acting jobs. At least not easily.”

“One of the unfair parts of the business.” He gave my hand a squeeze. “I doubt you’ll ever have to worry about—”

A gunshot rang out.

Brock tackled me to the ground.

Shutterbug ducked and whined, then took off like a bullet toward the road.

I wiggled out from under Brock, bolted to my feet, and raced after my dog. Brock caught up quickly, staying glued to my side.

We darted into the parking lot and toward Shutterbug’s high-pitched bark. Lying next to a silver Mercedes was Junior Johnson. Blood soaked his shirt, spreading across his shoulder.

“Call off your dog.” He groaned and got to a sitting position.

Brock rushed to help him. “What happened?”

“I don’t know. Someone shot me from across the street as I unlocked my car.”

I grabbed Shutterbug's collar and stared in the direction she barked. "Where's Detective Sawyer?"

Junior's eyes narrowed. "How should I know?"

"I thought since the two of you were walking along the beach together—"

"Stop bothering me and call an ambulance."

"My cell phone's in the bag," I said, patting my pockets.

"So is mine," Brock added.

"Use mine. It's plugged into the charger." Junior closed his eyes. "I think I'm dying."

"You aren't dying. It's a shoulder wound." I grabbed the phone and a small towel I found on the front seat. "Stay, girl." I let go of the dog, handed Brock the phone, then knelt down and pressed the towel against Junior's wound.

Brock took over applying pressure once he'd called 911. I moved to a nearby faucet and washed the blood from my hands. The pink-tinted water swirled around my feet before disappearing down the drain. By now, several people snapped pictures with their cell phones.

I frowned as I caught sight of Susan, a floppy hat on her head and a long cover-up swinging around her knees. She also took photos with her cell phone.

"Playing the hero again?" She raised her eyebrows.

"It saved your life, didn't it?" I rolled my eyes and turned back to Brock and Junior. I wasn't a hero. Heroes weren't afraid of danger. They embraced it. I, on the other hand, would do everything I could not to face danger again while

trying to find out who killed Ben.
How naïve could I possibly get?

CHAPTER FIVE

Detective Lawrence marched toward us, her face like granite. Behind her, Detective Sawyer squealed to a stop and exited his vehicle. He trotted to catch up with his partner and arrived next to us red-faced and sweating.

"Miss Canyon, why do you always seem to be at the center of things gone wrong?" Lawrence narrowed her eyes.

Sawyer eyed Shutterbug with suspicion, causing my dog's already present growl to deepen.

I shrugged. "Just lucky, I guess."

"Hmmm. Don't go anywhere." The detective moved to Junior's side and bent over to say something to him.

I stepped next to Brock and leaned my head on his shoulder. "At least he wasn't murdered," I whispered.

"Although, I'm sure it wasn't for lack of trying," he said.

"What do you mean?" I glanced up at him.

"Just that he isn't very well-liked. Someone did shoot at him. They missed making it a kill shot. Whether on purpose or not, we don't know."

"Why isn't he liked?" Lawrence appeared behind us like a ghost. "What makes you say that?"

We turned. "You're like a ninja," I said.

She gave a thin-lipped smile. "It's amazing what you learn when no one notices you. Why isn't this man liked?"

"Do you know who he is?" Brock frowned.

"Of course, I do. His father owns half the studios." She crossed her arms and glanced to where paramedics loaded Junior into the back of an ambulance.

"Johnson Senior also gives his son anything he wants." Brock swept his hand through his hair. "Junior has been into drugs since his teen years. Some people have suspected him of embezzling money from the studio, but it hasn't been proven. He's a rich snob who thinks he's entitled to everything."

Lawrence tilted her head. "You sound as if you have a personal issue with the victim. Where were you when he was shot, Mr. Hanson?"

"Sitting on the beach with Kelly." He crossed his arms, matching her stance.

"He was with me, Detective." I put what I hoped was a calming hand on Brock's arm. "We heard the shot, Shutterbug barked, or maybe it was the other way around…anyway, once we heard the shot, we ran this way."

"Into danger?" She raised her eyebrows.

"We thought someone might need help." Now, all three of us had crossed arms and stared each other down like dogs waiting to snatch a bone set in the middle.

"Are you going to interfere in my investigation, Miss Canyon?"

"I'm thinking of asking questions to write another book. I think a series about Hollywood murders might be a big seller."

"If you interfere, I will arrest you despite who your father was." She spun and left, joining her partner in the parking lot. They got into their cars and drove separately, presumably to question Junior.

"That woman is impossible." I snapped my fingers for Shutterbug to follow and headed through the parking lot to the car. Then, remembering our things, I veered left and caught up with Brock.

We gathered our beach items in silence until after we'd buckled our seatbelts in the car. Brock sighed and turned to me. "You're really going to write another book? I'd hoped you were kidding. Can't you write fiction and make stuff up?"

"I guess I could, but I really think I'm onto something here. People are fascinated with the lives, and deaths, of movie stars."

"You take pictures, you act…you're afraid of getting killed like your father…and now you're going to purposely get involved in a murder investigation." He shifted sideways to face me. "Did I get it right?"

"Pretty much." I forced a grin. "I'm trying to decide what I want to be when I grow up."

"For crying out loud." He turned the key in the ignition and roared onto the highway.

Everything he'd said was true. I did have a lot going on in my life and was scared to death of being murdered. Some people might say I had PTSD or was it PTSS now? I couldn't remember. Either way, being chased through a studio jungle by a mad woman wielding a gun had traumatized me. I figured helping solve Ben's murder was like getting back on the proverbial horse.

When Brock stopped in my driveway, I asked, "Are you coming in for dinner?"

He shook his head. "I have some thinking to do. I'll see you at the studio tomorrow."

"Ok." Pain welled in my heart. I motioned for Shutterbug to get out of the car, then watched Brock drive away. Would he stop seeing me if I continued with my plan? Would I stop snooping if he said he would?

"Why'd he leave?" Ruthie called from the porch. "I made lasagna."

"He's mad at me." I shuffled up the walk.

"Why…" She pointed at my shirt. "…is he mad, and why do you have blood on you?"

I glanced down. Sure enough, the hem of my bathing suit cover-up was stained red. "Junior Johnson was shot, and I had to stop the bleeding. Brock is angry because I told him I wanted to investigate and then wvrite a book about Ben's death. Book two in the *Hollywood Murders*."

"Macabre." She held the door open. "It's just us tonight. Doug has other plans. It's a good thing lasagna freezes well."

I headed straight for the shower. When I'd washed off the grime of the day and dressed in shorts and an oversized t-shirt, I forced myself downstairs. All I wanted to do was curl up in bed and mourn what I might have lost. Instead, the object of my heart waited for me at the foot of the stairs. My heart sank. "Are you here to tell me you want nothing to do with me?" I blinked back tears.

He sighed. "Not seeing you would be like ripping my heart from my chest and stomping on it." He held out his hand. "Care to talk to me?"

I put my hand in his and let him lead me to the back patio. A soft breeze blew, dispelling some of the heat of the day. We settled onto a wicker loveseat. I curled against Brock's side and waited.

"I'm sorry," he said. "I have no right to tell you what to do. You scare me, Kelly Canyon, in so many ways. For most of my life I've been self-absorbed. Oh, I know I'm a nice guy, and I'll help anyone in trouble if I can, but I've never wanted for anything or had anyone go against my wishes. I've been a spoiled brat ever since my parents realized my potential as a star."

"You're so far from spoiled, Brock."

He shrugged. "Not really. When you didn't agree not to interfere in Ben's death, I got mad. Again, it isn't my place, and you don't have to do what I say. So…" he smiled down at me, "partners again? Except this time, we aren't clearing either of our names."

"As long as you promise not to break your leg again."

"You have to promise not to be alone with any

suspects."

Technically, I hadn't been alone with Amber since Susan was with me, but I agreed. "I promise."

He tilted my face to his and kissed me, gentle at first, then with increasing pressure until I felt as if I'd melted into the hardness of his toned body. We pulled apart at the sound of a throat clearing behind us.

Detectives Lawrence and Sawyer stood in the doorway. I'd been so engrossed in my conversation with Brock, I'd not noticed them step outside.

"How long have you been standing there?" I asked, straightening.

"Long enough to know it's only a matter of time before I arrest you for obstruction of justice," Lawrence said.

Sawyer remained stony-faced.

I rolled my eyes. "Why are you here?"

"Junior Johnson said the two of you grilled him and caused him undue distress. He wants to press charges."

"What?" I leaped to my feet. "We quite possibly saved his life, the ungrateful—"

Brock put a hand on my arm. "We stopped the bleeding and asked him whether he knew who had shot him. That's all. There was no way to apply pressure without causing pain."

"I understand that," the detective said. "I'm just letting the two of you know that he might cause some problems for you. Stay out of my investigation, Miss Canyon. You too, Mr. Hanson."

"Would you two like to stay for lasagna?" Ruthie called out the door. "I made plenty."

"No, ma'am. We're on duty." Lawrence motioned her head toward the car, and the silent Sawyer followed her back through the house as obediently as Shutterbug did me.

I met Brock's gaze. "Why would Junior act like this?"

"I have no idea, but I plan on finding out. We helped him. I expect at least a thank you. Want to pay him a visit tomorrow?"

"Sure, but the least amount of time spent in that man's presence, the better."

We entered the house and took our seats at the table. Ruthie had set out three plates, a pan of lasagna, a plate of thick garlic toast, and a salad. The kitchen eating nook smelled divine.

Once we were settled and eating, Ruthie asked, "so you're going ahead with this, are you? Then, I guess we are now the Three Musketeers of crime solving. We should learn all kinds of useful things in the television series we're doing. I read the script." She waved her fork at us, causing a leaf of lettuce to fall onto her plate. "All sorts of law stuff."

I laughed. "You do realize that television isn't real life, right?"

"There's always some truth in fiction, Kelly."

"The more people involved, the bigger chance of the killer discovering what we're doing," Brock said.

Ruthie shook her head. "The more people, the safer it is."

They were both right, and I should have kept my mouth shut and gathered notes for my next book by myself.

CHAPTER SIX

"**Why do you dislike** Junior Johnson so much?" I asked the next afternoon as Brock drove us to the hospital. I was tired from filming the same scene umpteen times because Ruthie didn't agree with the way the scene was directed. I laid my head against the seat back and turned to look at Brock. "Lawrence is right. You seem to have a personal, rather bad feeling toward the man."

His shoulders slumped. "It's not something I'm proud of."

"I'd still like to hear about it."

"Did you know that he wanted to be an actor?"

I shook my head.

"When I landed my first leading role, Junior was my competition. I got the part, he didn't. The man did everything he could to discredit me, everything from saying I was a woman beater to a drug addict. When no one could prove his claims, my fans stayed true. There's been bad blood between us ever since."

"Is he capable of murder?"

Brock cut me a sharp sideways glance. "He's never shown a violent side before. He's just mean and spiteful."

"He won't be happy to see us then."

"Probably not."

Brock found an empty parking spot halfway across the lot, then hurried to open my door. We'd left Shutterbug with Ruthie with promises to fetch her as soon as we were finished with the unpleasant business of the day. I was hoping to gain a clue in addition to an apology, but wasn't holding my breath for receiving either one.

A nurse behind a desk directed us to Junior's room. The man sat up in bed, his right arm in a sling, and with a bored expression on his face, he scrolled through the available television channels. He scowled when he noticed us. "What do you want? Haven't you done enough damage? Here to finish the job?"

"We did nothing but help you." I put my hands on my hips. "You owe us an apology for filing a complaint with the police and wasting everyone's time."

His brows lowered. "Are you threatening me?"

"Of course not." I glanced at Brock. "What did I say that could be construed as a threat?"

"Nothing, Junior is just being Junior." Brock moved closer to the bed.

Junior reached for the nurse call button. "I'll press it, don't think I won't."

Brock held up his hands. "We're just here to get

an apology."

"You aren't getting one, and stop calling me Junior. I'm not a child. You pressed harder on my shoulder than necessary in order to cause me more pain."

"Next time we'll let you bleed out," I muttered.

Brock took a deep breath. "Let's change the subject. Do you know who shot you?"

"If I knew that, they'd be behind bars. Now, go away."

I could act like a child as well as the next person. I plopped into a vinyl chair. Air whooshed from the cushion. Crossing my arms, I said, "I'm not going anywhere until you say you're sorry and stop the complaint."

"I can have the nurses kick you out." He reached for the button again.

"Come on, man." Brock exhaled heavily. "We're just trying to see whether you getting shot is related to the death of Ben Jones."

Junior blinked like an owl. Obviously, the quick switch of subject matter left him speechless. "I don't know who that is."

"Yes, you do." I examined my fingernails which were in dire need of a manicure. "I saw you leave an abandoned building a few minutes before he did."

"You're mistaken."

I shrugged. "Once I develop the film, we'll know for sure."

His eyes widened. "You took my picture?"

I gave a slow nod.

"Fine. I'm sorry. I really am sorry for calling the

cops. Look." He grabbed the bedside phone. "I'm calling them right now." He asked for Detective Lawrence, said he'd overreacted from shock, and was dropping the charges. By the time he'd finished, I was dragging Brock out of the room. "Hey! You get rid of that film."

I pretended not to hear. It didn't take a genius to know that once Junior had placed the phone call to the authorities, he'd want a promise from me in return. I left before he could ask.

"We accomplished what we went for and gleaned a clue." I grinned up at Brock.

"What clue?"

"That Junior lied about being in the building with Ben."

"Maybe he didn't know Ben was there."

"Maybe." I increased my pace across the parking lot. "I'd like to go to the building and see if that's possible."

"Okay. Thank you for not going alone."

Brock parked around the corner from the abandoned building and in front of a drugstore. "We don't want anyone messing with my car."

I agreed. Hand in hand, we took an alley to a street much seedier than the one we'd left. "I caught sight of him over there."

"Why were you here, anyway?"

I lifted my shoulders. "Taking pictures. The gym is right there, and celebrities come and go all day." I smiled. "I saw you, didn't I?"

He laughed. "Yes, you did." He led me to the door and peered inside. "It looks deserted."

"I have a feeling it's early morning or late

evening when people come around."

"Let's hope so."

We stepped into the dim recesses. The afternoon sun highlighted floating dust particles dancing around its beams.

The corner of a tattered sleeping bag peeked through the doorway opposite us. Broken shards from the front window lay scattered at our feet. Despite someone's attempt to board the broken window, several planks had been yanked loose and now sat propped against the wall. That's probably how the visitors had climbed in at first, then waltzed out the front door leaving its lock battered and unusable.

I slipped free of Brock's hold and stepped through the opposite door. Several sleeping bags littered the floor along with hypodermic needles, razor blades, and dirty compact mirrors. "How can anyone do anything in this place? It's a breeding ground for disease."

"Are you sure Junior and Ben came from this building?" Brock held himself stiff as if moving would cause him to contract some fatal illness. "I don't see it."

"You're free to look at the photo." I scanned the walls. Another door hung loose on its hinges across from me. Two more doors branched off a short hall. I entered and found myself stopped by a heavier door. Using the hem of my shirt to turn the knob, I opened the door and stepped outside. "Maybe Ben entered through here and watched whatever Junior was doing. Maybe Junior really didn't know he was there."

"What would possess a man with Junior's wealth to frequent such a place?" Brock shook his head.

"Maybe his dealer?"

"The man could come to his house."

"Or woman." I stepped back inside and closed the door. Whether it made sense or not, I'd taken a photo of Junior leaving here and then Ben. Connected? I was sure of it. Was Ben killed because he'd been seen? That was what I intended to find out.

"Are we done here?"

I laughed. "Scared of a little dirt?"

"No, but I don't like germs, and I feel as if I'm breathing in tons of the little killers." Brock put a hand over his mouth and nose. His eyes twinkled. "My snobbishness is showing."

"Such a delicate man." I caressed his cheek. "Yes, I'm done here. Although I do want to return again with my camera."

"Not without me."

"My brave germaphobe."

Laughing, we exited the building, coming face-to-face with a very satisfied-looking Susan Gilroy. "I never would have thought I'd see the two of you frequenting a drug house." She motioned for her cameraman to snap a picture.

"We don't frequent this place. I'm following a lead." I brushed past her.

"A lead?"

Uh-oh.

"You're solving another murder? Is it that janitor's?" Her heels tapped a fast beat as she tried to keep up with us. "Can I help?"

"No." I reached for the car's door handle.

"Why not?"

I whirled. "Because you weren't any help when our lives were on the line. If not for me, you'd still be there curled up into a ball."

"I can handle danger now." Her eyes flashed.

"No." I yanked open the door, got in, and slammed it shut as Brock's door echoed mine.

He stared past me at Susan. "It isn't good to piss off the paparazzi."

"I don't care. Now she'll print it in the paper, that one—we were in that building, and two—I'm investigating again. Either way, the killer will be tipped off and Detective Lawrence will come knocking on my door."

CHAPTER SEVEN

A week later I stood in line at the grocery store wishing I could sink into the tile floor and out of sight. Staring at me from the cover of *The Hollywood Tribune* was a very clear photo of Brock and me exiting the drug house. The title read "Lovers' Rendezvous or Secret Addiction?" Seriously, Susan needed help in the title department.

Not wanting to get caught again, I hadn't returned to the building to snoop around. Maybe it was time. I had a flashlight and rubber gloves in my car, just in case.

Thankfully, I wasn't a big enough celebrity to garner attention, at least I didn't think I was, but plenty of shoppers were gossiping about Hollywood's Golden Boy. One misguided article and Brock's halo was tarnished. I sighed. It wouldn't be too long before someone else took the spotlight.

"Hey, it's Kelly Canyon." A heavyset woman waved one of the tabloids. "Will you sign this?"

Within seconds, autograph seekers swarmed me. "This article isn't true," I said.

"Of course not," the woman said with a grin. "It's all fiction made up to sell papers. Oh, some people might believe it, but I don't." She thrust the paper and a pen at me.

I felt a little better at her words, but from the hard glances sent my way, there were plenty of people who did believed the article. I pasted on a smile and signed papers until no one was left. Then, I loaded my groceries on the conveyor belt and paid.

As I left the store, two women followed, chattering like mockingbirds about how certain people thought they could do anything they wanted with little regard to moral principle. I sighed and put my bags into the trunk of my car. Without glancing their way, I slid into the driver's seat and drove home.

On the way, I called Brock on my Bluetooth. "Do you want to check out the drug house tonight?"

"In the dark?"

"Yes, it'll be easier not to be seen. Have you seen the tabloids?"

He groaned. "Yes. My agent is giving me flack about tarnishing my reputation."

"So, dark it is?"

"Dark it is. I'll be by later to pick you up."

Ruthie arrived home as I was putting away the groceries. "Let's have Brock over for a game night with Doug."

"We can't. We have plans."

"Where are you going? Doug and I can go, too."

"Nope." I set a carton of eggs on the top shelf of the refrigerator, then closed the door.

She narrowed her eyes. "Why not? Oh. You're going snooping! I want to go. I'll call Doug and cancel." She reached for her cell phone on the counter.

"Not this time, Ruthie. Please. We're going to the drug house, and I don't want you to be seen just as your career is reviving."

"I'll wear a disguise. This is too exciting to resist." She rushed away.

I followed her to her room. "What if we run into someone violent?"

"Brock will be with us. I'll take my pepper spray."

"You have pepper spray?"

"Yes, I gave you one." She dug in her nightstand drawer. "Oh, no, I didn't. I put it here and forgot." She tossed me a pink pepper spray canister. "See? We'll be perfectly safe, and it will help us get more into character for our show."

"Your logic defies all reason."

"Go dress in black and make sure you cover up your blond hair." She stepped into her cavernous closet.

By the time Brock arrived, I had dressed in a black t-shirt, black jeans, and wore a black cap on my head. Ruthie wore similar attire. Brock's eyes widened at first glance, then he shrugged. "I'm beginning to realize it doesn't pay for me to ask questions."

"Smart man." Ruthie patted his cheek on her way to his car.

"I'm sorry, but she was persistent," I said.

"No worries. The more the merrier, right?" He grinned.

"Not in this case." I slid into the front passenger seat.

"I made sandwiches." Ruthie passed out ham and cheese sandwiches. "You can't head into possible danger on an empty stomach."

"Thank you." Brock's grin widened as he bit into his and backed the car out of the driveway.

"Mustard?" I hated mustard.

"Oh, here's the one with mayo." Ruthie switched with me.

I couldn't help but feel as if she looked at the evening ahead of us as a great adventure, a party of sorts. "Grandma, I'm going to need you to settle down and be a little more serious. There will quite possibly be addicts at this place. We do not want to be seen or heard. Our only goal is to gather information. Not to make contact."

Brock laughed. "You sound as if we're talking about aliens."

"They might as well be." I laughed along with him.

Our gaiety faded as the sun set and Brock parked behind the drugstore again. "We'll enter through the back," I said, turning to face Ruthie. "No talking, no flashlights. Not until we find out if we're alone."

"I'll be as silent as a feather floating on the wind." She winked and shoved open her door.

I exhaled heavily. Since my grandmother seemed overly accommodating, I couldn't see the evening ending well at all.

We entered through the back door. Brock took the lead and held up a fist signaling us to stop.

"What does that mean?" Ruthie hissed. "The fist."

"It means to stop. Seriously, how did you get to be your age without knowing some things?"

"I've never been in the military, Kelly."

Brock sent a warning look over his shoulder.

We clammed up and moved forward. Voices drifted from the front room.

"Someone's been here," a man said.

"They'd better not be trying to take over our crib," another responded.

"Nothing's moved. It looks like they passed through."

"I don't like it. What if the cops are watching this place?"

"Let's vacate for a few days and let things cool." Footsteps receded, a door squeaked closed, and all grew silent.

"Stay here," Brock whispered.

"Take this." Ruthie shoved her canister of pepper spray into his hand.

He gave a slight shake of his head and stepped into the front room. "You can come in."

"Someone boarded up the front window," I said, clicking on a flashlight. The light's beam showed little else had changed except fresher footprints and a half-smoked joint left lying next to a sleeping bag.

"I guess they plan on coming back for that."

Ruthie pointed. "I bet they don't stay away for a few days after leaving that here."

"Shh. I can't think." I retraced my steps and veered right. That door led to a bathroom that emanated an odor strong enough to make me gag. I could not believe people actually used it in that condition. I pulled the door tight and tried the other door. Stuck.

I put my shoulder against it and pushed. It opened a couple of inches. I pushed harder, finally forcing it open enough for me to squeeze through. As I did, the back door to the building slammed shut.

I froze, waiting for someone to say something. I could hear Ruthie's and Brock's low murmurs from the front room. Shaking off my fears, I shined my light across a room piled with boxes. A storage room of some kind. Not unusual except for the fact the boxes looked new and undisturbed.

Another door slammed.

Ruthie screamed.

"Just the wind, I think," Brock called out.

Although no one was there to see me, I nodded and reached for the closest box. File folders upon file folders. I lifted one out. Ruthie Canyon was typed on the label. Inside were headshots, tabloid articles, and press releases. Further examination showed the boxes were full of actors and actresses who had signed under the studio label. An odd place to archive files.

A whiff of smoke teased my nostrils. I sniffed again, then stepped back into the hall.

"I smell a fire," Ruthie said. Her flashlight cast

an eerie glow on her face.

"I do, too." Brock moved beside her. "The front door is bolted from the outside."

Fear clogged my throat and I rushed to the back door. It wouldn't budge. Silver tendrils of smoke drifted under it. "We're locked in."

"Someone set fire to the building?" Ruthie clutched at her throat. "Why?"

"I found an archive of files of stars from the studio. It seems strange that they would be stored here. Maybe they were put here and forgotten. I did have trouble opening the door." I shined my light into the room I'd exited.

"Or maybe someone put them there in order to search them for blackmail." Ruthie's light joined mine. "Did anyone bring a cell phone? I left mine in the car. Nowhere to put it wearing yoga pants."

I patted nonexistent pockets. "Brock? The smoke is getting thicker. We need to call for help. Can you get the boards off the window?"

He tossed me his phone and made a dash for the front of the building. "The smoke is getting thick in here, too. Don't touch the door handles." He coughed and gripped one of the boards. "Find something to help me pry these loose."

I dialed 911, stated our emergency, and handed the phone to Ruthie. Then I scanned the room. Nothing. I headed for the file room. Nothing but paper and boxes. "I can't find anything." A fit of coughing overtook me. My eyes burned from the smoke, and tears ran down my face.

I joined the others in the front room and gripped a board with Brock. Together, we tugged until it came loose. I'd hoped for fresh air. Instead, heat blasted us in the face as the wall blazed. I pulled my shirt over my nose and gripped another board. It splintered in my hands. Shards of wood pierced my palms. Ignoring the pain, I tossed the board to the side, then bent over in another fit of coughing.

"The operator said to get down. Firemen are on their way." Ruthie slid to the floor.

I glanced at Brock, who nodded, then did the same. Tearing the boards off the window did nothing but cause smoke to billow in faster. Whoever had set the fire knew exactly what they were doing.

The three of us sat huddled close, shirts over our noses and waited for rescue or to die from smoke inhalation. I gripped one hand of each of their's and held tight.

Why would someone set fire to the building? Had they known we were in there? Was the fire set because of us or the files in the back?

Questions whirled through my head like the twister in *The Wizard of Oz*. The welcome wail of sirens alerted us to the fact help was on the way.

CHAPTER EIGHT

A fireman with an axe broke through the front door and waved us toward him. We crept forward and darted to freedom.

Someone ushered us into a waiting ambulance and placed gas masks over our mouths and noses. I gulped in the cool oxygen. My throat stung from the smoke.

A paramedic set me on the bumper of the ambulance and got to work on my hands, pulling out splinters, then cleaning and wrapping them in bandages. Due to the fear of being burned or suffocating, I'd managed not to dwell on the pain. Now that my attention had been brought back to my hands, they throbbed.

With a roar, the roof of the building fell in, shooting crimson sparks into a black velvet sky. Whatever reason the files had been stored there no longer mattered. There would be nothing to save once the fire was through.

As the paramedic finished with me, Detective Lawrence stormed in my direction. "Miss Canyon, you do not listen when I talk, do you? What were you doing in this building?"

"Trying to find out why William Johnson, Junior and Ben Jones were both seen leaving here a few minutes apart the day before Ben was killed." I forced the words from a raw throat.

Her features hardened. "Your interference could have gotten you killed."

"But it didn't. Do we know how the fire started?"

She glanced to where several firemen stood. "Considering a gas can was found by the front door, arson is suspected. Whether you were the target or not is under question."

I told her about the files. "Do you think they could have been the target?"

"There's only one way to find out. I'll be paying a visit to both Mr. Johnson, Senior, and the owner of this building. My guess is they are one and the same. Heed my warning, Miss Canyon. This is strike two."

I knew what would happen at strike three, and I also knew Ruthie would bail me out of jail. I fully intended to find out who owned the building for myself and determine who stored those files.

I slept until ten a.m. but woke to the ringing of the telephone. "Hello?"

"You're late. We were supposed to film today. You're costing me money." Click.

Uh-oh. Louie was cantankerous on his best days. On his worst, well, I felt like calling in sick. Instead, I crawled out of bed and woke up Ruthie. An hour later, we stumbled into the studio.

Loui frowned. "You look like something that crawled out of a sewer. Why isn't your makeup done?"

"Gee, thanks. We wanted you to know we were here first." I plopped into my desk chair. At least, the desk chair for the show, anyway.

"You can't film with bandages on your hands. Today's an active scene. You have to point a gun."

I stared at him. "Film a different scene. How about the one where I'm sitting behind my desk?"

"There isn't one!" He threw down his clipboard and stormed through a set of double doors.

"Does this mean we aren't filming?" Ruthie glanced in the direction he'd left.

I shrugged. "Let's see if he comes back." I folded my arms on the desktop and laid my head down. "If he does, we'll have Lisa do a quick fix to our faces."

I must have fallen asleep because I woke to someone tapping me on the head with a pencil. "What?" I glared at Louie.

"Let me see your hands."

I groaned and unwound the bandages. The cuts were minor. "I suppose I can grip a gun." If I could stay awake long enough.

"Get this woman coffee and find the makeup gal." Louie marched off again. "Where's Ruthie?"

She popped up from a sofa against the far wall. "Here."

"What were you two doing last night to be so tired?"

"Painting the town a fiery red." She grinned. "We'll be ready to film within the hour."

"You'd better be."

The day's filming was a nightmare. I couldn't hold a gun with my sore hands, at least not with any degree of believability. If I tried to grasp the weapon firmly, my hand throbbed. By the end of the day, everyone, including the perky Lisa, was in a foul mood. The bright spot of my day was Shutterbug waiting patiently for me to take her home.

"I want everyone on the set and ready to go by six a.m." Louie waved his arms around as he paced. With a final glare in my direction, he stormed out the door.

I snapped my fingers for Shutterbug to follow me, then headed to the trailer I shared with Ruthie. Since my grandmother was in conversation with one of the beverage girls, I wasn't waiting. I wanted to lie down ASAP, take a nap, then go home and sleep some more.

"Wait up." Ruthie rushed in my direction.

"You're awfully chipper for little sleep and a long day."

"I found out something," she sang. "Something about Ben Jones."

Suddenly awake, I grabbed her arm and yanked her behind a storage building. "I'm listening."

"The drink girl, Lacey, I think her name

is…maybe Lucy. Anyway, her name tag is smeared—"

"Ruthie!"

"Right. Yes. She said she heard Ben and Rod arguing the night before Ben was killed."

"About what?"

"Money." Ruthie wiggled her eyebrows. "She said she couldn't help but overhear because she was stocking bottles of water in the cooler when they came in. Louie wanted them chilled and ready for the next day's filming. They'd already started arguing and she didn't want them to be embarrassed that she was there. So, she sat down and waited."

"Sounds like eavesdropping to me."

"I'm not judging her."

I waved a hand. "Continue, please. Were any names mentioned?"

"No, but she said they were definitely arguing about someone who had coerced someone else into some kind of money-making scheme."

I crossed my arms and leaned against the building. "I wonder who. I'm thinking out loud here, but it sounds as if Ben either overheard about the scheme or was involved directly."

A can rattled nearby.

Shutterbug let out a deep bark.

Ruthie and I ducked. When no further sound came from the other direction, we continued to the trailer where Lisa banged around her supplies.

"Your mood didn't improve," I said, realizing taking a nap was out of the question now.

"Louie seems to think it's my fault the two of you were late. He has now informed me that I am to act as your alarm clock." She put her fists on her hips and stomped her foot. "I insist you set your own alarm clock and be on time."

"We'll do our best," I said, grabbing my camera bag from the closet I'd set it in that morning.

"Not good enough so far." Lisa snatched her purse from the counter and stormed from the trailer.

"People sure are upset with us today," Ruthie said. "Let's decide what to have for dinner."

"Something simple. Tacos?"

"We'll pick some up on the way."

"I'd like to talk to Lucy before we go. Do you know where we could find her?"

Ruthie thought for a moment. "The staff building?"

I knew where that was. I'd spoken to Ben and Rod several times outside of it a few months ago. "It won't take long."

"I'll wait for you here. Take your dog. I'm going to sleep." She spread out on the sofa and closed her eyes.

I yawned with envy. With my dog trotting at my side, I headed to where Rod smoked alone in the spot he'd once shared with a friend. He wore a baseball cap cocked to one side over gray hair in need of a haircut. Perfect. I'd speak with him, too. "Hey."

"Hey." He motioned toward the folding chair next to him. "Sit a spell."

"I will, thanks."

"Nice dog." He lit a cigarette and gazed at Shutterbug who sat next to me as still as a statue.

"How have you been, Rod?"

"Slim to fair. Things aren't the same, you know?"

"I'm sure they aren't. May I ask you a question?"

"Sure."

I took a deep breath. Rod was a nice man, but I was asking more difficult questions than I'd asked in the past. "I heard you and Ben argued the night before he died."

"Who told you that?"

I pressed my lips together.

"You and your secrets." He shook his head and straightened in his chair. "Yeah, we got into a real big argument. Ben said he heard two men talking about how they were going to bribe people with information hid at some drug house. That they'd be richer than they'd ever thought possible. I told him to stay out of it."

"He wanted to be a part of the bribe?" I now knew why the files had been stored in that building.

"No, he wanted to confront those responsible."

"Did he tell you who?"

He shook his head. "I told him it wasn't any of his business, and sticking his nose where it didn't belong would get him killed. Looks like I was right."

Someone other than myself knew Ben had been in that building. "I'm sorry, Rod. I know you two were close."

"Just find his killer, Miss Canyon. I know that's why you're asking questions." He held up a hand when I started to speak. "I don't care what your motive is, I only care that justice is served for Ben."

"I'll do my best." I stood. "Please don't tell anyone we spoke. I'd rather not have a mad man chasing me again."

He chuckled. "I won't say a word."

"Thanks." I opened the door behind us and went in search of Lacey/Lucy. Mary, one of the women who cleaned the trailers, waved upon seeing me. I headed her way. She'd know where the woman was that I looked for.

"I think you mean Lindsey," she said. "She's the only one with a name like that. She might be in the staff lounge getting ready to leave if she hasn't already. If you need something, I'd be happy to get it for you."

"That's all right. I need to ask her a question. If she's gone, it can wait until tomorrow." I smiled my thanks and headed for the lounge.

From the quizzical looks on the few faces in there, they weren't used to non-staff stepping into their private domain. "Lindsey?"

A dark-haired woman around my age of twenty-five glanced up from where she traded gym shoes for heels. "That's me."

"Do you have a minute?"

"For what?"

"I have a question." The four people's eyes darted from her to me to Shutterbug and back to Lindsey. "In private?"

"I guess, but it will have to be quick. I have a date." She grabbed a floral, oversized bag and sailed out the door, leaving me to follow. I practically chased her to the parking lot before she stopped. "If this is about the necklace, I found it in the garbage."

"I'm not here about that." Although, if she found it in the garbage of a star's trailer, it might be construed as having fallen in accidentally. I shook my head. "I'm here about a conversation you overheard."

She paled. "I'd rather not talk about it."

"Why not?"

"Because a man died."

"That wasn't your fault."

"Yes, it was. If I would have interrupted them, then maybe Rod wouldn't have killed Ben."

"What makes you think that?" Rod would be the last person in my mind to have killed, but friends have murdered friends before.

"Who else?" She opened the door of her orange Kia and tossed her bag inside. "It's always the closest person to you."

"Not always. If Rod did kill Ben, then you letting them know you were there would only have put you in danger."

Her brow furrowed, then she grinned. "You're right. I did the smart thing by staying silent."

"No names were mentioned during their argument?"

"Not a one. Just that someone stole some files from the studio and wants to get rich by bribing people."

"Do you know where the files are kept?"

"I know where they were at one time." She slid into the driver's seat. "They used to be in trailer twenty-one, but they disappeared months ago. I really do have to go."

"Thanks." I glanced in the direction of trailer

twenty-one. I'd have to make it over there sometime soon.

CHAPTER NINE

"You want a photography session today? For how many poodles?" I grimaced, almost forgetting I'd put out the word weeks ago that I would do portraits for pets. That was before I'd accepted the acting job. It was all money in the bank, but I hadn't expected someone to call and schedule before the sun was up, though.

"I have twelve assorted sizes," the woman said, as if dogs were pieces of art décor or table settings. "They are very well-behaved, I assure you."

Which meant they were monsters. "I'd love to, Mrs. Rogers. How does six o'clock sound?"

"Perfect." She rattled off her address and hung up.

"Well, Shutterbug, how do you feel about the French? You are German after all." I laughed and ruffled the fur around her neck.

I'd wanted to visit trailer twenty-one after shooting for the day, but those plans would have to wait. "I'm getting nowhere fast on finding Ben's killer."

Shutterbug gazed up at me with soulful eyes.

"Why can't you find something as critical to the case as you did when you were a puppy?" Months ago, she'd found a pair of shoes with incriminating red paint planted behind the victim's laundry basket. The very woman whose house we now owned. Finding those shoes had set us on a quick path to discovering my makeup artist was a cold-blooded killer. All in the name of fame.

My cell phone rang. "Hello."

"This is Lisa, your friendly wake-up call. You have thirty minutes to get here." Click.

"Wow, that girl takes her job seriously." I quickly donned street clothes and yelled for Ruthie as I darted through the too-large-for-two-people mansion. "I'm taking a shower while your makeup is getting done. You're first!"

"I'm already dressed." Of course, she was. My grandmother stepped out of the kitchen with two travel mugs of coffee in her hands. She wore a flowing caftan style dress that only she could make fashionable. Easy on, easy off, she'd said more than once. She handed me one of the mugs. "Let's take the convertible."

"Really? You've never let Shutterbug in it before."

"She has proven herself to be a very good dog." Ruthie smiled at my girl, then sailed past us and into the garage.

"Oh, girl, you are in for a treat." I rushed after Ruthie, Shutterbug on my heels.

I switched the dog seatbelt from my car to the passenger seat of the 1965 Candy Apple red convertible Corvette and snapped Shutterbug in. Then, I slid into the driver's seat and sighed. I loved this car. Ruthie rarely drove but kept it in mint condition.

She handed me the keys, her eyes sparkling. "It's yours."

I laughed. "I always drive."

"No, I'm giving you the Corvette."

"What?" Tears sprang to my eyes. "Do you want my Volkswagen?"

"No, I have the Camaro. You keep this. The Volkswagen can be your work car, this one is for pure pleasure." She squeezed onto the seat next to Shutterbug and ran her hand over the dash. "When I do ride in it, you drive, so I might as well give it to you now rather than in my will."

My heart stopped. "Are you ill?" I whirled to face her. "Are you dying?"

She gave a head-back, full-throated laugh. "Not for a long time, I hope, and you call me the dramatic one."

"I love you, Grandma."

"This time, I'll let you call me that." She planted a kiss on my cheek. "Now, drive before Lisa has a coronary."

I think Shutterbug enjoyed the ride as much or more than I did. Her head hung over the doorframe, tongue hanging out, ears back, hair blowing. This car was the best gift I'd ever been given.

I parked at the far end of the lot to keep people from dinging the car, when they opened their door and put the roof up. Then, I opened the trunk and took out the vinyl cover Ruthie never used.

"Good grief. If we have to go through this every time we go somewhere," Ruthie grumbled, "we'd better leave a half hour earlier. That seatbelt barely fit over me and the dog. Next time the three of us go anywhere, we take the Volks or the Camaro. I'm covered in dog hair."

"Go on ahead. I'm hitting the shower anyway." I wouldn't be rushed in taking care of this old beauty.

We made it to filming on time. Louie looked shocked but pulled himself together and immediately started barking orders. By the time lunch arrived, I had a headache. I filled a plate from the buffet table in the back and headed to the picnic area outside.

"Brock." I grinned at seeing him there. "Are you waiting for me?"

"Yes." He stood and pulled out my chair. "At least I hoped your lunch break would be around the same time as mine. How's your day?" He leaned over and gave me a slow, deep kiss.

"Hmm. Started off wonderful, got rocky, then shot back to wonderful with that kiss."

"Good." He smiled and dug his fork into a large chef salad.

"How's your day going?"

"Filming is smooth. I have to run from an exploding building, and the director keeps wanting to do it over and over. I'm going to be sore tomorrow."

"Why don't you use a stunt double?"

He frowned. "At twenty-eight, I'm perfectly capable of running and falling on my own."

"Just don't mess up that pretty face." I popped a strawberry into my mouth. "Want to come with me tonight to photograph twelve poodles of assorted sizes?"

"Heck no. That sounds like torture, but for you, I'd do anything." His eyes darkened.

"Thank you." My face warmed, and not from the noonday sun. "I'm sure I can use the extra set of hands. Ruthie gave me the Corvette."

"Really?" His eyebrows rose. "That's wonderful. Why?"

"She said I'm the only one who drives it. Something's up her sleeve, I think, but I have no idea what."

"She and Doug are pretty chummy. What if they're making wedding plans?"

My fork paused halfway to my mouth. The chicken salad plopped back to my plate. "You really think so? Have you heard something?"

"Not really. Would it be a bad thing?"

I thought for a minute. "No. She deserves to be happy, and that chubby little man makes her happy."

At five-thirty, I loaded my photography equipment into the Volkswagen, clipped Shutterbug into the backseat, and waited for Brock to arrive. Five minutes later, he pulled into the driveway and we were off to take pictures of chaos.

Mrs. Rogers was a tall, thin, well-dressed woman with coal-black hair and bright pink lipstick. Her makeup made the light-blue sheath dress looked less stylish. Yapping and running in circles behind a fenced enclosure in her massive living room were poodles from tea cup size to standard.

Shutterbug froze in the doorway. Her hackles rose.

"Shh." I put a hand on her head. "These are our clients."

She settled, but her eyes remained on the largest poodle. A beautiful, silver male. I sincerely hoped my dog wasn't in love.

"Where do you want my babies?" Mrs. Rogers asked, thinly tweezed eyebrows arcing toward her hairline.

"Do you have a preference?"

"Outside by my hydrangea bushes."

"All right." Nightmare waiting to happen. How were we going to get this many dogs to sit still?"

"Leashes," Brock whispered in my ear. He surprised me by how often he could read my mind. "We'll secure the dogs to whatever is stable, and you can photoshop the leashes out of the picture."

"You're a genius!" I grabbed a pile of leashes from a wicker basket beside the door and followed Mrs. Rogers to the back yard.

"I almost didn't hire you after seeing the picture of you coming out of that drug den," she said, "but after asking around, I found most people said it was impossible for the rumors to be true."

My steps faltered. "Thank you, I guess."

"I realized you were most likely researching

another book. Am I right?"

I nodded, narrowing my eyes. What was she getting at? I handed the leashes to Brock, leaving the roundup of groomed pets to him. "I'm considering it."

"Good, because I thoroughly enjoyed the first book. My niece let me read the advanced copy. She reviews books in her spare time, you know." She sat in a wicker chair and propped tanned legs on an ottoman. "I know everything there is to know about Hollywood. Maybe I can help."

"Do you know who killed Ben Jones?"

"Unfortunately, I do not. I'm sure it has something to do with a letter I received." She lifted a black envelope from the table next to her. "It's typewritten." She handed it to me.

I opened the envelope to see a photo of a young Mrs. Rogers in an incriminating position with Louie. That man did get around. I read the short typed note. "I want twenty-thousand dollars. I'll be in touch. Comply or suffer disaster." Creative. I looked closer at the photo, recognizing the younger version of Mrs. Rogers. "You're Olivia Rogers, Academy-Award winner actress for *The Teacher*."

She smiled. "That was years and years ago, but yes, that's me. I have no idea why someone would want to blackmail me about something that happened so long ago. Louie was nothing but a stagehand then." She chuckled. "I did like the younger men."

"Have you contacted the police?"

"I just received the letter last week. I was waiting for this person to get in touch again. That's why I think it has to do with Ben Jones. I received the letter, he died, and no more contact."

I handed it all back to her. "You may be right. I'd put this somewhere safe and contact the police immediately if you get another letter." I hurried to where Brock had the dogs amazingly settled.

Assorted colored rose bushes added beauty to the photo, and I snapped photo after photo of the dogs being still, licking each other's ears, wagging their tails…everything that dogs do. When I thought I had enough pictures, I helped Brock unhook the poodles from the leashes. They exploded across the lawn as if they'd escaped the dog pound.

I assured Mrs. Rogers that I would deliver quality photos in her requested sizes in seven to ten days, then I said, "Be careful. It's quite possible it wasn't Ben Jones who mailed that threat." The kind man didn't seem the type.

"Don't worry about me, sweetie. I've twelve protectors." She lifted the blond teacup poodle. "I have a state-of-the-art security system."

Back at the car, I told Brock about the letter the client had received. "So, that is what all those files were for." He picked up his phone and sent a text. "We'll know soon who owns that building."

"With transients in and out, it could be anyone working with the killer."

"Yes, but it is a place to start."

"The files used to be kept in trailer twenty-one. I had planned on going there tonight, but Mrs. Rogers scheduled an appointment. I'm rather glad she did, considering."

Brock nodded. "We'll make it to that trailer at

the first opportunity. Right now, I need to shower off dog hair."

"Poodles don't shed."

"Oh. Well, I feel as if they do." He flashed a grin and sat in the passenger seat.

We entered the house to a silent Ruthie sitting very still on the sofa.

"What's wrong?" I rushed to her side. It wasn't like her not to greet me when I came home.

She held up a black envelope over her head without turning to look at us. Scattered across the coffee table were pictures of a younger, very inebriated Ruthie.

CHAPTER TEN

"I guess that means Ben wasn't the one doing the bribing," I said.

Ruthie shook her head. "Why would someone care what happened more than twenty years ago? It can't hurt my career now."

"Olivia Rogers received a letter, too." I sat on the sofa next to her. "I guess all we can do is wait for you to be contacted."

"What other files were in that room?" Brock asked.

"I only saw Ruthie's, but there were a lot of boxes." I glanced at Brock. "Anything in your past that might come to light?"

He slumped into a chair. "There's an ex-girlfriend that might show up, but I can't see that being a reason for blackmail. Everyone has an ex."

"Since Olivia isn't the only one receiving the letter, we need to call Detective Lawrence. I also doubt Olivia and Ruthie are the only ones. We just don't know about the others." I idly scratched Shutterbug behind the ears. How could we find out whether anyone else had been threatened? Old-fashioned pounding the pavement and outright asking, I supposed.

I pulled out my cell phone and called Detective Lawrence. "We've had a threat. Can you come?"

"You're investigating and getting into trouble again."

"This has nothing to do with me."

"I'll be there in ten minutes." Click.

While we waited, Ruthie poured three glasses of wine. "Whether you like it or not, take a glass. We can all use it."

Her tone left no room for argument. I took a sip and grimaced. Still, the warmth from the drink settled the churning in my stomach. By the time Lawrence arrived, I'd relaxed a bit. Threats were nothing new, but the last time they were directed at me, not my grandmother.

I shook my head when Ruthie attempted to refill my glass. She shrugged and sat down, leaving me to answer the door when the bell rang.

Lawrence stood on the front porch, this time without her partner. "Where's the threat?"

"Come in." I opened the door. "My grandmother received a black envelope and an old photograph with a note." I led her into the living room and pointed at the table. "She isn't the only one. I had a photoshoot at Olivia Rogers' house this evening and she also had a note like this. I'm guessing there are more stars being blackmailed."

Lawrence pursed her lips. "Why do you think

that?”

"Because before the drug building caught fire, I found boxes and boxes of files on celebrities."

"Which ones?"

"Well…I only saw Ruthie's file, but I'd bet the others were the same." I crossed my arms, realizing how much speculation we had to go on. "Have you discovered who owned that building? You might as well tell me, because we'll find out. Brock has already asked an acquaintance to look into it."

She sighed. "William Johnson, Senior." She snapped a pair of vinyl gloves on her hands and slipped the note, envelope, and photo into a paper sack. "I'll be paying Mrs. Rogers a visit next. Do not tell anyone you've received this threat, and do not pay the twenty thousand. Let me know the instant you receive contact." She speared us all with a glance. "Understood?"

We nodded in unison. Although, not saying anything would make it difficult to ask questions of others. She didn't say not to say anything about Mrs. Rogers. I smiled.

"Whatever is going through your head, Canyon, you can forget about it." With those words, the detective slammed the door behind her.

"Busted," Brock said, laughing. "You were trying to think of a loophole to snooping without actually going against the detective's orders, weren't you?"

"Yes." I returned his grin. "She said nothing about questioning other people or mentioning Mrs. Rogers."

"Same thing." Ruthie gathered up the glasses

and headed to the kitchen.

I resumed my seat on the sofa. "Other than Ben, Junior was the only one I saw at that building. We know there are others because we heard them. Any idea how we can find out who was there before the fire was set?"

"Nope." Brock sat next to me and propped his feet on the coffee table. "You really need to make a connection with someone in the police department. There might be videos of people coming and going from there."

He had a point. Maybe I could get one of my father's old buddies to help us out. "There is one sergeant getting ready to retire. He worked with my father back in the day. I can ask him, but if he says no, he might tell Lawrence."

"Are you willing to take that chance?" Brock studied my face.

"I think I might be." Yes. I nodded. I would take that chance if it kept someone from harassing Ruthie.

"I'd best be getting home." Brock leaned over and kissed me. "I can see myself out. Want to meet for lunch again in-between filming?"

"Most definitely. It will be the best part of my day." I'd decided I really wasn't a fan of acting. I loved the money, but the work part was a real drag.

Louie was in a good mood during filming the next day, so the day ended early. With Shutterbug's leash gripped firmly in my hand and her service dog tag in plain sight, I entered the police station and asked the receptionist if Sergeant Dixon was available.

"Who's asking?"

"Detective Canyon's daughter." I smiled.

She spoke into a phone, then told me to head back to the last room on my left. I cast a worried glance into Detective Lawrence's office, relieved to see she wasn't there, and entered Sergeant Dixon's office.

The portly man smiled and stood, offering me his hand. "If it isn't little Kelly all grown up. Sit a spell."

I shook his hand and sat across from him.

"How are you?" His smile didn't fade. "As you can see, I've been delegated to a desk, but with retirement approaching, I'm not complaining."

"I'm acting now. Still taking pictures."

"I always thought you'd follow your father into law enforcement."

I lifted my shoulders. "I dabble. In fact, that's why I'm here." I filled him in on everything that happened, beginning with Ben's death.

"Yeah, I heard about that. I also heard how you helped catch that movie star's killer." He shook his head. "There's a lot of bad people out there, Kelly. If you aren't on the side of the law, it's dangerous."

I cleared my throat, then told him of Ruthie and Olivia receiving the threats. "I'm wondering if you'd have access to the videos around that old building that burned down."

He sat back in his chair and crossed his arms. "I might, but I seriously doubt those cameras are working. That's a rough part of town, and most of the time, the cameras are just for show, but I'll see what I can do." He folded his hands and laid them on the desk. "Detective Lawrence is a tough cookie. She won't like you messing in her investigation."

"I know. She asked for my help the last time, then backed off when danger approached." I stood. "I'll be more careful this time. I can't wait for action when the danger is to Ruthie."

"I understand. You are definitely your father's girl." He grinned. "Write down your phone number and I'll call if I find anything."

"You're the best." I scribbled my number on his desk pad and headed home.

Brock waited for me on the front porch. In his hand he held a black envelope.

"Yours?"

He nodded. "Yep." He showed me a picture of him and a pretty redhead. It was obvious they were arguing, and Brock's hand was raised as if he were going to strike her. "This was printed in a tabloid early on in my career. Sharon was helping me practice for a part and paparazzi snapped the photo. A lot of people actually thought I hit her despite her insistence that I didn't."

"This could definitely tarnish your halo."

"It could ruin my career."

"Let's pay a visit to trailer twenty-one right after filming tomorrow. There has to be a clue as to who took the files," I said, putting a hand on his arm. "Don't worry, Brock. We'll get to the bottom of this."

CHAPTER ELEVEN

The poodle portraits were finished. I smiled looking at the antics of the dogs. Some even seemed to have been grinning when I snapped their picture.

Wait a minute. I squinted and held the photo closer to my eyes. Someone had watched the photo shoot from the protection of the hydrangea bushes. I made a photocopy of the picture and slid it into my bag to take to the police station later. "Come on, Shutterbug." I snapped my fingers. "Let's do a better job of letting me know when someone is lurking about, okay?"

She panted and trotted for the door.

"Some ferocious watchdog you are. Shouldn't you know what do at almost seven months old?" I hooked her into her seatbelt, trying to avert my face from her kisses. "What if I was in trouble? You should be more like Lassie." I laughed, closing the door.

"Lassie, huh?" Brock stood behind me, arms crossed, dimple winking. "Where are you headed?"

"To deliver Mrs. Rogers' photos. Look." I pulled out the one I'd enlarged. "What does that look like?"

"A set of eyeballs." His eyes widened.

"Yep. Want to come?"

"Wouldn't miss it." He jumped over the door and into the passenger seat like an action hero. The man was too sexy for words without even trying. It astounded me that he wanted to spend time with me.

Olivia met us at her front door. "I got another one." Tears welled in her eyes. "They said if I don't deliver the money tomorrow night, they'll hurt one of my babies."

"We won't let that happen." I put my arm around her and steered her to the sofa. "Did you call the police?"

She shook her head. "I just checked the mail a few minutes ago."

"Where do they want you to go, Mrs. Rogers?" Brock perched on the edge of the coffee table and took her hand in his. She seemed to calm under his gaze.

"I'm supposed to give the money to Spider-Man on the Walk of Fame next to my star."

"Which Spider-Man? There are usually several."

Her chin quivered. "I guess I'll know."

"I'm calling Detective Lawrence." Brock patted Olivia's hand, then stepped onto the back veranda.

"I've got something to cheer you up." I glanced up to see Brock strolling across the lawn toward the hydrangeas. "The pictures have been developed."

"Wonderful." She reached for the thick folder. "I'm sending my babies to stay with my sister in San Diego. I can't chance anything happening to them."

"I understand. I'm quite attached to my fur baby, too."

Olivia decided to purchase all of the photos and ordered some in different sizes. "Let me write you a check." She wrote one for five hundred dollars, then left the room, returning a few minutes later with a cardinal red briefcase. "I need to go to the bank. Can you see yourself out?"

"You can't give into their demands, Olivia." I stood. "Once you do, they'll never stop."

"I'm not going to be harassed or live in fear, Kelly."

"Look. Ruthie and Brock both also received letters." I cringed, knowing Detective Lawrence would be furious at me for not following her order. "You can't tell anyone. We don't want to tip off the blackmailer."

"They're not going to pay?" Her eyes widened.

"No, ma'am."

The doorbell rang, sending twelve poodles and one German shepherd into a frenzy of barking. "Shutterbug! You know better." I opened the door to see Detective Lawrence and Sawyer pulling gloves onto their hands. I let them in.

Sawyer held back, his wary gaze on my dog while Lawrence sat next to Olivia. "Let me see the letter," Lawrence said.

While the two of them talked, I moved outside

to where Brock had eased behind the hydrangea bushes. "It's a tight fit," he said, "but someone definitely stood back here. Check out the muddy footprints."

"I'll take a look."

I gave a shriek and whirled, not realizing that Sawyer had come up behind me.

Sawyer's mouth twitched. "Sorry."

Somehow, I didn't think he was. "You shouldn't sneak up on people."

He blew a puff of air out of his nose. "What are you two doing?"

"Checking for footprints." Brock exited the bushes. "Show him the photo, Kelly."

"I'll show him and Lawrence both, so I don't have to go over it twice." I made my way back across the lawn. The moment I opened the French doors to the house, Shutterbug darted out and immediately took up position by my side. "I'm sorry, girl. I shouldn't have left you behind."

I could hardly get into the house with her pressed so close to my legs. The dog seemed determined to stay between me and the door, or was it Sawyer that made her hackles rise? She didn't like him, and he was very wary of her. I blew out a breath. There were more important things to think about than who my dog didn't like.

"She's got photos," Sawyer said, moving to the other side of the room. "Hanson was crawling in the bushes."

"I wasn't crawling." Brock scowled and sat in a white leather chair.

"Explain, please." Lawrence looked at me.

"When I was photographing Mrs. Rogers' poodles, someone was watching. I noticed this after developing the film." I handed the detective the extra photo. "You can clearly see eyes and part of a face through the branches."

She studied the photo, then handed it to Sawyer. He stared, frowned, and handed it back. "Yep, that's a face."

"Do we know whose face?" I asked. "The eyes appear to be blue, but they are in the shadows."

"Blue eyes don't give us much to go on," Lawrence said. "You have blue eyes, Hanson has blue eyes, Sawyer has blue eyes…most of Hollywood has blue eyes. It could have been a nosy neighbor for all we know."

Mrs. Rogers shook her head. "None of my neighbors would dream of hopping my fence for fear of my fur babies."

"They weren't very good at warning you someone was watching." Lawrence slid the photo into a folder she carried.

"They were distracted by Shutterbug and having their picture taken." High spots of color appeared on the older woman's cheeks. "My dogs are normally quite protective. Now, what are we doing about the blackmailer's demands?"

"We'll be there to nab them with that red bag full of fake bills." Lawrence glanced at Sawyer, who nodded. "If none of you tip them off, we'll be able to close the case quickly."

Mrs. Rogers hugged the smallest dog to her chest. "What about the letters Brock and Ruthie received? Have they received the blackmailer's demands?"

Lawrence whipped around to face me. "Can you not follow a simple order?"

I grimaced. "I tried."

"Not very hard." She turned back to Mrs. Rogers. "There's no need for you to worry about the others, ma'am. You have enough to deal with. We'll be back tomorrow before the scheduled meeting time to finalize details."

"You mean…I have to go?" Her eyes widened.

"The perp will be watching for you, ma'am."

"Oh, dear. Well, I'm taking Prince with me. There was no mention of me not taking a dog."

I assumed Prince was the largest of the bunch, and I didn't blame her. In her spot, I'd do the same.

Mrs. Rogers sighed and got to her feet. "I'd better schedule a hair appointment and a manicure. I refuse to die not looking my best. Please see yourselves out." She headed down a hallway and disappeared into a room.

The four of us stared at each other, then left. I found myself rarely surprised anymore by the eccentricities of Hollywood's stars.

"Would you want your hair done before facing a potential killer?" Brock asked as he drove home.

"Not really, although I was dressed up when Amber chased me."

"That's because you were kidnapped from Lauren's memorial party."

"Then, to answer your question, I wouldn't care what I looked like. The mortician would make me up to look like anyone but myself anyway." Morbid conversation. "Can we change the subject?"

"Sure. Sorry. I was just curious. Some women are very strange."

I laughed. "Now, you're learning. I have a question for you now. It's only a matter of time before you and Ruthie also get a demand for money. We need to start digging for someone who needs cash."

"That could be anyone."

"I think we should concentrate on those who work in the studio. It has to be someone who had access to the archive files. That wouldn't be a random person off the street."

He rubbed his hands up and down his face. "You're right. It has to be an actor or a crew member. I hate that the studio is going through this again. If I hadn't signed a contract, I'd consider going to a different studio."

"Really?" I'd never considered that idea. Ruthie had spent her entire acting career in the same place where she now reinvented her career. I'd assumed I would do the same until I became a photojournalist. Or an author. I still hadn't really decided what to do long term, but I'd told myself when I started acting I'd know for sure by the age of thirty. That left a little over four years.

"I'm assuming we're going to be watching for Spider-Man tomorrow night?"

I grinned. "You bet. We can't let Lawrence see us though."

"I know a gift shop near there that will let us loiter."

I cut him a sharp glance. "You know where Olivia's star is?"

"I do. She was my grandmother's favorite actress. I took her to see the star before she died."

"Great. We'll be there to grab him in case he slips away from the cops."

CHAPTER TWELVE

"Oh, this is just like in the movies." Ruthie clapped her hands.

"Shhh." Brock had been called to a promotion for his upcoming film, leaving me stuck with my talkative grandmother since I promised not to snoop alone. I didn't consider Shutterbug with me as being alone, but I was outnumbered. "We're incognito. Detective Lawrence will have our heads if she discovers we're here."

"We'll just tell her the truth. We're here to support Olivia."

I rolled my eyes. That excuse wouldn't work in the slightest. I checked my watch. Fifteen minutes until Olivia was to show up at her star. Three Spider-Men posed for photographs. Our only hope was that one of them would approach her.

Shutterbug growled deep in her throat as a fourth Spider-Man arrived, this one wearing a costume that had seen better days, and said something to the others that caused them to move further down the sidewalk. We had our perp. Now we waited for him to take the purse when offered.

Ruthie grabbed my arm. "Let's go grab him."

"Not until he takes the money, and only...I stress only...if he evades the cops. Then, we cut him off and help the capture. We don't know for sure that he's the one we're looking for."

"There's Olivia!"

Dressed in a bright purple dress and carrying the requested red bag, Olivia strolled down the sidewalk with not only Prince, but all twelve of her dogs, tugging at their leashes and stopping to sniff every object and person they passed, marking their spots every few feet. It would take her forever to reach where she needed to be.

"Come on," I muttered.

Finally, she stopped on her star, set down the bag, and turned to greet a couple of fans who recognized her. Within seconds, a crowd had formed, blocking our view of Olivia, the bag, or Spider-Man.

I stepped around the tree I'd reclined against, grateful for its shadowy protection and rushed toward Olivia as Lawrence and Sawyer hurried from the other direction. We met in the middle of the fans. No bag. No Spider-Man.

"We'll talk about you being here later," Lawrence promised before taking off at a sprint in the opposite direction.

With a firm grip on Shutterbug's leash, I darted after her. Ruthie had gotten involved in the whole autograph signing, leaving me free to follow the detective.

"Find him, girl." I let Shutterbug loose. She liked most people, but she'd growled when this particular superhero wannabe came into view. "Hold him."

The dog shot off, quickly bypassing Lawrence, who I caught up with. She cut me a sideways glance, gave a nod, and kept up the pursuit. "You really should consider becoming a cop."

"No, thanks."

"If you did, I wouldn't have to threaten you with arrest."

Threaten being the operative word, I grinned and stopped to catch my breath.

Shutterbug's frantic barking spurred me back on. She had poor Spider-Man hugging the outside wall of a small restaurant.

I snapped my fingers and motioned for her to come to my side as Lawrence moved toward the masked man. "Get your hands up," she ordered.

He did as he was told.

By then, Sawyer, heavily panting, joined us. "You girls are fast."

"I ran track in high school," I said, shrugging.

Lawrence pulled off Spidey's mask. "Who are you and why are you blackmailing people?"

A young man around twenty-years-old shook his head. "Not me! I was paid one hundred dollars to grab the bag and not get caught. I'm Jason Wells." He glanced at the bag lying in an oily puddle. "What's in the bag?"

Sawyer grabbed it. "None of your business." He glared in my direction. "This is police business,

Canyon. Out."

"Fine, but if it weren't for my dog, you would never have caught this guy." I hooked the leash back on Shutterbug's collar and went to find Ruthie.

I found her and Olivia sipping coffee in a corner café. "I love being back in the spotlight." Ruthie's face glowed.

"It's where you belong." I fell into the empty chair.

"Well, did they get my money back?" Olivia leaned forward. "Who was it?"

"A hired kid, and yes, Detective Sawyer has your money." I patted Shutterbug's head. "My girl nabbed the thief." Maybe I should add loaning my dog to the police as yet another career choice.

"I can't thank you two enough." Olivia's eyes shimmered. "It was an adventure, but I'm too old for such things." She stood and unlooped the dog leashes from the back of her chair. "I'll spread the word to all my friends about your talent as a pet photographer, Kelly. I have two right now that will want them for sure. One breeds Yorkies and French mastiffs. Can you imagine? What a difference in size and temperament. You'll be busier than you can imagine. I'll write their numbers down. Tell them I sent you." She smiled and strolled away, head high, hand gripping the leashes.

"I asked her why she brought all the dogs," Ruthie said. "She said it was because they were her family and made her feel safe. Then, with Shutterbug catching that crook…well, I'm starting to think dogs aren't too bad after all."

"Now that I've had my girl, I can't imagine how

I lived without her."

"I think she deserves a treat. Let's go home and give her two cookies."

"Dog ones, I hope."

"She loves oatmeal."

"Grandma!"

"I've asked you not to call me that." She grinned. "I'm kidding, Kelly. Of course, they're dog cookies."

Brock was waiting on the porch when we returned home. "I'm anxious to hear all about it. Did you catch the guy?"

I grinned. "Shutterbug did. Come in and I'll tell you."

We laughed, talked, kissed, and talked some more until late into the night. Brock's promotion had gone well, with him and the leading actress signing autographs and posing for pictures. So well that they wanted him to pretend to be in a relationship with the leading lady. He'd refused, which made me warm all over.

"There's only one leading lady for me," he said, giving me another kiss. "See you tomorrow?"

"I don't have any filming."

"I was thinking about a day at the beach." He grinned.

"It's a date." I walked him out and practically floated up the stairs to my room.

Shutterbug's scratching at the bedroom door woke me. I shuffled down the stairs to the back door and let her out. "Hurry up." She never had to go out in the middle of the night.

She returned almost instantly with a raw steak in

her mouth and dropped it at my feet.

"Where did you get this?" I crouched down. There was no way Ruthie would have dropped a steak in the backyard. We hadn't grilled out there in a long time and this T-bone looked fresh. "You really are a smart girl, aren't you?" Using the tips of my fingers, I lifted the steak and dropped it into the sink before calling Detective Lawrence.

"I think someone tried to poison my dog."

"Canyon?" From the grogginess of her voice, I could tell I'd woke her.

"Yes, it's me. Luckily, Shutterbug is very well trained and brought the steak to me." The obedience lessons I'd taken her to a couple of months ago were worth the money. "She woke me up several hours earlier than she ever does to go outside and then returned to drop a T-bone at my feet."

"I'll be right there." Click.

"Since Shutterbug is technically a service dog," I said later after letting Lawrence into the house, "she knows not to eat anything that isn't given to her by myself, Ruthie, or Brock."

"Service dog for what?" Lawrence rubbed her eyes.

"I do believe I'm suffering from PTSD after the whole Amber thing."

She cut me a quick look. "So, not an official service dog."

"Good enough for me. Let me show you the steak in question." I led her to the kitchen, Shutterbug close on my heels. "The blackmailer had to be there when Shutterbug cornered that kid. He saw how handy she was and tried to get rid of her."

My throat clogged.

"We don't know that, although she is a smart dog who did something we couldn't." She narrowed her eyes. "Despite the fact her owner was somewhere she shouldn't have been." She stared into the sink. "Do you have something I can put that in to take to the lab?"

I got her a plastic container and lid. "Sorry, no paper bags."

"This is fine." She dropped the steak into the container. "I'll let you know the minute I hear something."

"What happened to Spider-Man?"

"He's spending the night in jail until he's ready to tell us who hired him. He still says he doesn't know. Business was conducted over the phone."

"Burner phone?"

Lawrence nodded. "We won't be able to hold him longer than twenty-four hours."

"How does someone who wants to hire him get ahold of him?"

"By asking around. Good night, err, morning, Canyon. Take care of this dog." Without waiting for me to walk her to the door, she left.

I locked the door behind her and headed back to bed. A tantalizing aroma wafted into my dreams. Bacon! I threw off the sheet I'd covered with and thundered down the stairs. "What's the occasion?"

Ruthie turned from the stove. "I've decided we're cutting out carbs. We can eat as much bacon as we want."

"But, I don't want to cut carbs." I'd always been able to eat whatever I wanted without gaining weight.

"I won't be successful unless we're both eating the same thing." She returned to cooking.

I groaned and sat at the table. Taking a deep breath, I told her of Shutterbug finding the steak.

Her back stiffened and she slowly swiveled toward me. "Are you saying that someone came onto our property and purposely tried to kill our dog?"

"It appears that way. Detective Lawrence will let us know for sure once she knows."

"What about the guy they arrested?"

"Seems he was hired over a burner phone." I propped my chin in my hand.

"Then I guess we need to call on the friendly neighborhood Spider-Man."

CHAPTER THIRTEEN

On this trip to the Walk of Fame, Brock insisted on coming with Ruthie and me, my grandmother refusing to be left behind. Shutterbug came along as protection. She might only be eight months old, but my little girl had grown very big and very loyal. On the other hand, Brock—the dream of many a movie-loving woman—didn't instill a lot of confidence in his ability to protect damsels in distress. But, he might surprise me.

I glanced at his muscled arms. He'd never been thrust into rescue mode, but I'd like to believe Brock would become my knight in shining armor if need be. Ruthie craved adventure. Me, well, sometimes I wondered where my head was.

I parked on the street a few spaces down from Olivia's star. "Look for the Spider-Man with a small hole in his left knee and a sun-faded costume who goes by the name of Jason." I shoved my door open and retrieved Shutterbug from the back seat of the Volkswagen she'd shared with Brock.

Ruthie, refusing to be slobbered on and me not wanting to drive the Corvette to a rough part of town, Ruthie had complained about being squashed the entire ride. "Thank the Good Lord above." She groaned and stretched. "My legs were cramping."

"Really?" I quirked my mouth. "You're no taller than my own five-foot-two, and I had plenty of room."

"You kept your circulation going by pressing on the gas pedal and the brake. It makes a difference."

I took my upper lip between my teeth to keep from smiling. "Well, I'm glad that's over for you. Maybe you should take a taxi home."

Her eyes narrowed. "Maybe I will."

"Ladies." Brock motioned his head to where a faded Spider-Man leaned against a building wall. "Showtime."

"Oh, no. Not that dog." Spidey turned and ran.

I sighed and unhooked Shutterbug's leash. "Hold him." She shot after the scared young man while the three of us sprinted after them.

People yelped and darted out of our way. "Sorry, sorry, excuse us," I yelled as we gave chase. Brock and I soon left Ruthie behind.

"I'll get coffee!" She called.

Spidey stopped in the doorway of a closed store. He bent at the waist and struggled to breathe. Shutterbug sat in front of him, her gaze fixed.

"What do you have against me, lady?" Spidey straightened.

"We just want to ask you a question." I clipped the leash back on my dog.

"You a cop? One of them K-9 ones?" He pulled off his mask and wiped his sweating face with it.

I shook my head. "I heard that a person needed a burner phone in order to hire you, but since I know who you are…"

"What do you want?" Cockiness replaced his fear. "I don't come cheap. Oh, and I don't kill people."

That was good to know. I pulled a fifty-dollar bill from my pocket. "Who hired you to take the purse?"

He eyed the money. "I don't know. They called me."

"Man or woman?"

"Man. Deep voice. Gruff."

It wasn't much, but it was something. "Can you get ahold of this person?"

He shrugged. "You've got to hand me that money if you want this conversation to continue."

I gave him the money. "Answer the question."

"I can if they didn't throw away the phone. Most people do."

"I'll give you one hundred dollars," Brock said, "if you get this person to contact us."

"By phone?"

"Either way." Brock scribbled my phone number next to his on one of his business cards.

"Hey!" Spidey grinned. "You're that actor. The one the girls call Brock Handsome."

Brock rolled his eyes. "You just now recognized me?"

"I was looking at the pretty woman, dude."

I grinned. "Yeah, Brock Handsome, he was

looking at me."

Brock smiled. "Let's meet up with Ruthie. Jason, no games. If we think you're trying to pull a fast one over on us, you'll not see that money and we'll tell the cops that you tried to poison her dog. You didn't, did you?"

His eyes widened. "What? No way. I said I don't kill people, and that applies to animals too, I guess."

"Good to hear." Brock went to clap the guy on the shoulder and Spidey ducked. "Sorry." Brock groused. "We look forward to hearing from you." He rested his hand on my lower back and steered me away.

"Do you think he'll call?" I asked.

"If we don't hear from him in three days, we'll come visit again." His arm moved to my shoulders. "Let's get that coffee."

Ruthie sipped a mocha drink when we joined her. "I didn't order yours because I didn't know how long you were going to leave me alone."

"Not a problem." Brock darted into the coffee shop.

"Sorry." I sat across from her. Shutterbug lay at my feet.

"Did you find out anything?"

"Spider-Man was hired by a man with a deep voice. He's going to try to get this man to contact us, although I'm not holding out much hope there."

"Well, I was very lonely here alone. None of my fans are around. I need to get me a pet, a service animal to relieve my loneliness."

"A dog?" My eyebrows rose. "You barely

tolerate Shutterbug. I guess if you got a small one—
"

"I was thinking of a miniature pony or a pig?"

"A pig!"

"Who's a pig?" Brock handed me my frozen mocha coffee.

"No one, dear. I'm thinking of getting one of those cute little pot-bellied pigs to carry around."

He blinked a few times. "They squeal."

"They're cute." She tilted her head. "It's either that or a pony."

"I doubt you can take either of those animals on a plane." I was going to call that Yorkie breeder first thing when we got home. No, even better. I'd drop Ruthie off and call on the way. She couldn't resist if she wasn't with me.

"Where are you going?" She asked when she got out of the front seat and Brock took her place while I stayed seated.

"I have to take Brock home."

"His car is here." She put her hands on her hips. "You're up to something."

I smiled and backed from the drive.

"So, where are we going?" Brock asked, clicking his seatbelt into place.

"To get Ruthie a dog small enough to fit in that big bag of hers." I shuddered, thinking of the alternative. "If not, she'll get something crazy."

He laughed. "I'm always up for an adventure with you."

"Olivia gave me the name of a breeder." I grinned. "I think I'll let Shutterbug choose the puppy. She'll have to live with it."

We drove to a ranch-style house with an unusually large yard for Los Angeles. Bought back when property wasn't such a priceless commodity, the sprawling white-sided house sat back from the street. I could hear the yapping of dogs before getting out of the car.

Shutterbug's ears stood at attention and she gave an answering bark. I barely attached her leash and detached the seatbelt before she lunged from the car. "Heel."

She gave me a sad look and sighed as if to say, "hurry up."

The front door opened before we stepped onto the porch. A woman as round as she was short opened the door, a friendly smile on her face. "Kelly Canyon? Olivia said you might give me a call. This is an unexpected pleasure. I'm Alice Steuben."

"My camera."

Brock held it out to me.

"Thank you." I turned back to Mrs. Steuben. "I came to purchase a puppy, but I'd be happy to photo them for you."

"Wonderful. You pick out the one you want, and we'll photograph the rest for my website. Even exchange?"

"Deal." I thrust out my hand.

She led us into a well-maintained backyard with a small dog run and a larger one opposite. I headed for the Yorkies, Brock for the mastiffs. He looked as happy as a little boy at Christmas.

Shutterbug sniffed the puppies, then licked the face of one feisty little gal so full of energy she couldn't sit still. She was perfect.

"We'll take this one," I said.

"And this big guy." Brock approached, a puppy with enormous feet tucked against him like a football. "I've always wanted a French mastiff, but never knew any reputable breeders."

"We're turning into a zoo." I said with a laugh.

Brock set his puppy down, and Mrs. Steuben fetched the little darling I'd chosen for Ruthie. The two younger dogs gamboled around Shutterbug, who looked on like an indulgent older sister.

"I'll pay for Brutus," Brock said. "Kelly can make the trade."

I almost choked when Mrs. Steuben said the puppy was two thousand dollars. "How much is the Yorkie?"

"We're making a trade," she said, "but this micro breed is in the thousands."

My eyes widened, my mouth dried up. "But I can't take nearly enough pictures to justify that cost."

"Look, Miss Canyon. Olivia and I have been friends since grade school. She called last night and told me how much the two of you have helped her. You get your puppy free, and Mr. Handsome here gets his at a discount. No arguments." She gripped my hand. "Truly, I appreciate you helping Olivia more than I can tell you. Maybe in some way, these two babies can help you solve crimes for those books you're writing." She winked. "You are writing more, aren't you?"

I nodded, speechless at her kindness. "Thank you. The dog is for my grandmother."

"Even more reason. Ruthie is a sweetheart."

I spent the next hour snapping photos of darling little puppies through the tears shimmering in my eyes. Sometimes the kindness of strangers did me in, turning me into a gushy mess.

Brock put his hand on my shoulder. "You okay?"

I nodded and sniffed.

"Mrs. Steuben is filling out the AKC papers. Want to take a picture of me and Brutus?"

"Sure."

Brock scooped up the puppy who tripped over his own feet as he lumbered around the yard. Brutus immediately started cleaning Brock's face. I snapped photos of Brock laughing, his hair messed, his shirt wrinkled, then one of him rubbing noses with his new best friend. I sighed. God had definitely broken a wonderful mold with this man.

Once the photos were taken and registered papers and pups were in our hands, we climbed into the car. The two puppies immediately tried to get in front with us. I raised the console, blocking them in the back. "We need more dog seatbelts."

Brock laughed. "You need a doggie hammock for that little one. She won't surpass two pounds fully grown."

"Perfect." I smiled.

"Oh, no." Ruthie rounded the corner from the kitchen at the exact moment Brock set Brutus on the living room floor. "Not another dog. What is that thing?"

"A French mastiff." Brock's face beamed.

Brutus immediately jumped on Ruthie. "Get this

monster off me. How big is he going to get?"

"Huge." Brock beamed as he moved the puppy away from Ruthie. "I'm turning him into a service dog, so I can take him everywhere."

"Here." I pulled the Yorkie from my purse and held it out. "I got you one too."

Ruthie's mouth fell open. "Look at those eyes. Oh, honey." She took the puppy in her hands. "Why, she's as light as a feather."

"She's perfect for your purse."

"That she is. Oh, this sassy little thing will be my service animal. Forget the pig."

"You three are taking this service animal thing for granted, aren't you?" Lawrence stepped from the kitchen.

"Is it wrong?" I asked. "It's ridiculously easy to get, and I'm pretty certain that not all of the dogs I see in the stores are there because of their owner's disability."

She lifted one shoulder. "I don't have a problem with it. I stuck around waiting to let you know the photograph of the eyes peering from the hydrangea bushes has disappeared."

CHAPTER FOURTEEN

Since I tend to go where I don't belong, Detective Lawrence immediately named me as her top suspect in the disappearance of the photograph. Early the next morning, I sat in her office, the desk between us, and tried to get her to see reason.

"Why would I steal the photograph when I have the negative?" I crossed my arms and leaned back in the chair. The detective had refused to let me bring Shutterbug into her office, so cooperation was low on my list.

The detective mimicked my posture. "You tell me."

"For crying out loud. Why don't you tell me why I'm really here?"

"Why don't you tell me why you were questioning our friendly neighborhood Spider-Man?" Her lips twitched.

I stiffened. "How did you find out about that? Do you have someone following me?"

"Maybe."

We had a stare-down contest for several seconds. I refused to give in first. Lawrence had a reason for me being there, and it didn't involve anything I'd done illegally.

She laughed. "I made an educated guess that you went back to see Jason Wells. So, what did you learn?"

"He's going to get ahold of the person who hired him and have them contact me or Brock for a possible job."

Her features hardened.

"What?" I did my best to look innocent. "It isn't breaking the law to have someone have someone else call you."

"You're getting very close to crossing that line." She sighed and shook her head. "I brought you here to ask if we could hire you to take photos. Our photographer up and quit on us, and you have a good eye, not to mention an incredible dog. But we'd only need you temporarily. Can you handle a crime scene?"

"You mean like blood and guts?"

She laughed again. "Not this time. A break-in. We should have a new photographer by tomorrow, but I'd like to use you as a backup. I've done a background check—"

"I didn't consent to that. You violated my privacy."

"So, sue me. Do you want the job or not?"

"When? I have filming tomorrow."

"Right now?" She stood.

I nodded, then went to fetch Shutterbug and my

camera bag from the receptionist. Minutes later, we followed Lawrence outside to where boxes had been dumped in a vacant lot. The wind had plastered papers against a chain-link fence. Yellow crime-scene tape encircled the lot. "What exactly am I looking for?"

"Anything out of the ordinary."

"You mean more than the police files floating around?" I set the exposure on my camera and started snapping.

"See? You've a good eye."

I rolled those alleged good eyes. "Anyone can see what's here." I still thought she had another motive for bringing me here and decided to wait until she was ready. After slipping on a pair of paper-thin booties, I moved around the lot, studying the vacant lot through my lens. Shutterbug, nose to the ground, headed away from me.

Since I could focus only on what showed in the small area, I could pick out what others might miss. Like the shiny button of an LA cop's uniform. I took a picture, then motioned Lawrence over. "Any reason this button would be in one of the boxes?"

"Maybe. One of these boxes held your father's reports."

I lowered my camera. "Why would someone be interested in ten-year-old cases?"

"That's what I'm trying to figure out." She squatted next to the button. "This still looks new."

"Why would it be in his case files?"

"It most likely wouldn't be." She straightened.

"Is there any way of knowing if anything is missing?"

"Not really. Keep looking, okay. You might find something else." She turned to walk away.

I shot out a hand and grabbed her arm. "I'm looking for something in particular, aren't I? Something you think only I would spot as being out of the ordinary. What?"

"I don't know." She glanced at the ground as if trying to determine how much to tell me, then fixed her gaze on mine. "I think one of the PD's finest is involved in the blackmailing."

"Who?"

"If I knew that, I'd arrest them." She shook her head. "It's just a gut feeling anyway. That photograph was taken from a locked room."

"Who knew you had it?"

"Everyone in the department."

Shutterbug let out a single shrill bark. Her clue that she'd found something. Lawrence and I hurried toward her.

A pair of feet encased in leather shoes stuck out from behind a dumpster. I lifted my camera and started taking pictures working my way around to the body. Leaning in, I took a picture of a very dead Junior Johnson.

"He's been shot at close range," Lawrence said. "Grab your dog and step back. I need to close off this area."

I inched around the perimeter of the lot, snapping more pictures of the pages I could see without touching or turning any over. I tried to think about which cases Dad might have mentioned within earshot of my teenage ears.

All I could recall were traffic stops, the

occasional robbery of a convenience store…nothing that would warrant someone dumping his case files in an empty lot in their desperate search for something. Not only his files, but others. Why? What could be so important someone would risk discovery by taking them?

I started paying closer attention to the dates on the pages I could see. They were all at least ten-years-old. "Detective."

Lawrence glanced over.

"Whatever they're looking for happened when my father was still alive. You might want to question any retired officers from around that time."

She smiled. "Good thinking. I'll look into it personally."

So, would I, but I wisely kept my mouth shut. Ruthie would know the names of the officers Dad worked with. It wouldn't be too hard to locate them, I hoped.

When I returned home, I told Ruthie what I'd found. Her shoulders slumped as they always did when Dad's death came up. She cuddled Sassy to her cheek. "I have a photograph here somewhere with your father's department. He wrote the names on the back."

I followed her to the office where she unlocked the antique roll-top desk my father had used. I'd loved watching him sit there in his leather chair, writing letters or paying bills. I missed him so much at times it left a physical ache in my heart.

"Here it is." Ruthie handed me a photograph of ten men wearing the uniforms of the LA Police Department. "This was before he made detective.

I'm not sure how many are still living or whether they're in California anymore."

"I can find out online. Thanks." I gave her a quick kiss on the cheek before heading to my room.

I leaned against the headboard, laptop on my lap, Shutterbug stretched out next to me, and started the hunt. After an hour, my legs fell asleep and my back hurt. Maybe I wasn't as good at Internet research as I'd thought. I leaned my head back. Did I know someone who was?

This might be a long shot, but Lisa owned a computer. I dialed her number.

"Lisa here. Hello, Kelly." Her cheerful voice made me smile.

"This is a silly question, but how good are you at looking things up on the computer?" Oh, please be trustworthy.

"I'm great, actually. I went to college to study computers, but decided I preferred doing makeup and meeting celebrities. Why?"

"I need help from someone with experience."

"Super. I'm free now. Do you want to meet at the trailer? It has good Wi-Fi service."

"Absolutely. I'm leaving now." I hung up, shouted to Ruthie where I was going, and raced to the car with my faithful companion at my heels.

Lisa already had her laptop ready to go when we arrived. As I took a seat next to her, setting up my own laptop, she rubbed her hands together. "So, what are we looking for?"

I handed her the photo. "These men. The names are on the back."

She flipped the picture over. "Friends of your

father's. Nice. Are you doing this as a gift for him?"

"He died ten years ago. I'd just like to find them."

"I'm sorry. Okay." Her fingers flew over the keyboard. "Why not order some Chinese to be delivered? I'm starving."

My eyes widened. "How will they get in?"

She cut me a sideways glance. "Serious? You don't know about the button?"

"Obviously not."

"Every building has an intercom with a button. Look on the wall next to the door."

"I thought that was a security alarm." My face heated.

"Now, you know. The delivery guy will arrive, show identification at the security gate, then announce himself to us. You tell him where to deliver and let him in. Simple.

I wondered why Brock or Ruthie hadn't mentioned anything, but then we'd never ordered takeout at the studio. The cafeteria suited our purposes. I placed the order, then settled back down to watch Lisa work.

"I've found two deceased so far. The other seven are proving a little harder. Why do older men not like social media?" Since she didn't look up, I figured she wasn't expecting an answer and kept silent.

I grew bored waiting and raced to the door when the food arrived. I stood in the doorway and watched a thin teenager rode his bike to the trailer. "Thanks." I paid him and carried the food inside.

"Great." Lisa pressed a button, and the printer

on the counter came to life, spitting out sheets of copy paper. "Let's eat while I tell you what I've found."

While she opened the boxes, I collected the printouts. There seemed to be one for each of the seven remaining men.

"One of them is a private detective now," she said, unwrapping a set of chopsticks. "Most of them seem to be enjoying the retired life, but one…" she pointed the sticks at me, "didn't like your father very much."

My heart skipped a beat. "What do you mean?"

"I hacked into some emails. Yes, I told you I was good. Your father had accused this man of stealing from the evidence room. Of course, nothing came of the accusations, but this Officer Moore threatened to make your father pay. I don't think he's one of the men you want to reminisce with."

Maybe not, but he is exactly the man I wanted to talk to. "Anything interesting with the others?"

"They all seem to be the buddies they appear to be in the photo." She pinched a shrimp with her sticks. "Things are not always as they seem, though, are they? One of the nice guys could be bad. That is the real reason you're looking for them, right? To find out something."

"Am I that transparent?"

She laughed. "Everyone knows you're writing another book. I'm interested in learning how these ex-cops related to Ben's death."

"Me too."

"I'm glad to help anytime you need snooping done on the computer." She grinned.

"I'll take you up on that." We enjoyed the rest of the meal in female chatter before parting ways.

Ruthie was anxious to hear what I'd discovered. I showed her the information Lisa had printed. "I remember an altercation between Kevin and this Moore. Your father was so enraged he was visibly shaking, but as far as I know, the issue was resolved."

"How was he acting before he was killed?"

She paled. "Are you thinking his death wasn't random?"

I shrugged. "I'm not sure his death is related to this case. I'm fishing in a very large pond."

"Hollywood isn't as big as you think. Everyone knows everything about everyone, even law enforcement. You just have to find the person who knows what you want to know and will talk."

CHAPTER FIFTEEN

I made a list of Dad's remaining law enforcement buddies and hoped one of them would be that person who knew what I wanted to know and would talk to me. Naturally, since I had somewhere I wanted to be, filming took forever. Take after take after take.

"Cut!" Louie bolted from his chair. "What is wrong with you, Canyon? If you don't act more forceful, that perp is going to shoot you. Act like you mean it!" He shook his head. "Actors. The bane of my existence."

"Sorry, I'm preoccupied." I resumed my stance and two-hand pointed my gun at my fellow actor. "Turn around! Hands up."

Since Louie didn't call cut, I figured I'd finally gotten the take as he wanted. Ruthie, my "mother," raced toward us. She clipped handcuffs on the man's wrists and took his elbow.

"Cut. Finally." Louie stood. "I hope you're

better equipped to do your job tomorrow, Canyon."

"I'll do my best."

He rolled his eyes and stormed off.

"I swear," Ruthie said, removing the male actor's handcuffs, "he's been even more unbearable since his wife left him. I didn't think it was possible for him to be worse. I need to find him a woman."

"Stay out of it." I kissed her cheek. "I'm headed out to interview the men on my list. Don't worry. I'm taking Shutterbug."

Her brow creased. "Do you want Sassy? She's great for warning you when someone is around."

"That's because she barks at everyone." I grinned. "No thanks."

She glanced around the room for her little darling, collected her from under the snack buffet, and tucked her into the quilted purse Ruthie had made just for the pup. "Suit yourself."

"Don't hold dinner. I'll grab something on the way." I looped Shutterbug's leash around my wrist and rushed to the Corvette. After buckling her in, I headed for a nearby retirement community to speak to buddy number one.

I entered a lobby where a purple-haired older woman sat filing her nails. "I'm here to see Mr. Robert Jenkins."

"Identification? And sign the roster."

I flashed my driver's license and did as instructed.

"He's in bungalow eight." She pressed a button without looking up, and a sliding door opened letting me onto a well-manicured lawn. The "bungalows," which were actually nothing more than apartments facing the lawn, were set in numerical order making number eight easy for me to find.

A tall, thin man with a receding hairline answered my knock. "What? I know you aren't selling anything because Wanda doesn't let solicitors in."

"I'm Kelly Canyon, and I'd like—"

He slammed the door in my face.

"That was rude." I glanced at Shutterbug, whose ears twitched. I pounded again.

"Go away. I got nothing to say."

"Please. Just a couple of questions."

What sounded like the volume to a television blared. Seriously? "Fine. I'll be back, though."

"I'll tell Wanda not to let you in."

I moved closer to the door. With the television that loud, he had to have his ear plastered against the door in order to hear me. "That won't stop me. I'm Canyon's daughter. That ought to tell you how persistent I can be."

The door opened. "Come in and make it quick."

I grinned down at Shutterbug, then ducked inside. Wow. I barely had room to walk through stacks of magazines and newspapers. "This is a death trap."

"It's my death trap." He plopped a folding chair down. "Sit down and start talking."

A foul odor came from somewhere to my right. I breathed through my mouth, fighting the urge to cover my nose. "Was my father onto something that would incriminate another officer?"

Jenkins crossed his arms and sat back, reaching

for a pack of cigarettes. "Why do you want to know?" He lit a smoke.

I prayed he wouldn't set the place on fire. "Because I'm investigating the murder of a maintenance man at the studio and I think—"

"You a cop?" He blew a plume of smoke into the air.

"No, an actress."

"One of those."

"Look, Mr. Jenkins, you're wasting our time. Do you know anything or not?" I narrowed my eyes and placed a hand on Shutterbug's head. She'd started getting jittery, feeding off my emotions.

He sighed. "Yeah, I know something, but not much. Your father suspected one of us was skimming off the top. He was focused on us more experienced officers, but I think it was one of the rookies."

"Why?"

"Because us ten were a brotherhood. We wouldn't have done that."

"Would any of you try bribing celebrities to make an easy buck?"

He laughed. "What kind of question is that?"

"Can I have a list of the rookies during that time?"

"Nope." He stubbed out his cigarette. "You'll have to find that out on your own. I'm not a snitch."

"Thank you for your time. I'll let myself out." I stopped at the door and turned. "Be careful, Mr. Jenkins. This apartment isn't safe." I stepped outside with Shutterbug and stared at the next name wondering if I was wasting my time. Maybe I should start with the rookies. They were most likely online somewhere.

The door behind me opened. "Speak with Morgan." Slam.

All right. He was number five on my list and lived a few miles away in a seedier part of town. The sun hung low on the horizon. I'd have to question him tomorrow.

I left through the front office, signing out the time. "Thanks."

The woman I presumed was Wanda again didn't look up. "Yeah."

"I guess that's the retirement center for rude people," I told Shutterbug, hooking her into the car. "I'm grateful for the little Jenkins told me, but it was like pulling teeth."

She licked my cheek and whined.

"All right, we're going home. We never did pick up something to eat."

I stopped at a fast food place and bought two quarter pounders. One for me and one for my girl. Halfway home, it became obvious someone was following me.

Now that the sun had set, I couldn't tell the color or make. Only that it was a sedan. *Please do not ram the Corvette.* I'd never get over anything happening to this car.

Rather than ram me, the driver behind seemed content to stay two car lengths back. I sped up. So did he or she. Had they followed me to Jenkins'? Should I drive home? Dad always said to drive straight to the police station, but since I suspected an officer was behind all the trouble, that didn't seem the wisest choice.

So, I drove along the Pacific Coast Highway, hoping the driver behind would get bored and leave once they figured out I was on nothing more than a pleasure trip. I pulled into the lot at Seal Beach just long enough for Shutterbug and me to eat, then continued our leisurely attempt at getting rid of the person tailing us.

My cell phone rang. I hit the speaker button. "Hello."

"Where are you?"

"Hey, Ruthie. I'm driving Highway 1 with some moron tailing me for the last hour."

"What?"

"Someone is following me. I'm not sure what else to do but bore them into leaving, I can come home."

"Go to the police station."

"What if it's one of them?"

She sighed. "Okay, but stay where there are other people. Turn around if you see nothing but vacant road in front of you."

I laughed. "In LA? Name a place devoid of people."

"All right, smarty pants. Call me if you get into trouble. I'll think of something to do to help."

I wasn't sure what she could do, but I appreciated the thought. Two minutes hadn't passed, and my phone rang again.

"Hello?"

"Come to my house." Brock's voice cut through the creeping darkness. "You'll be safe here. I can call Lawrence. You trust her, right?"

"That's a wonderful idea. I'm getting tired. See you in a bit."

"Be careful, sweetheart."

I smiled at the warmth in his voice. "I will."

I made a U-turn on the side of the highway and headed home. As I passed the sedan, I glanced over, but the tinted windows were too dark to see who was driving, so I grinned and waved instead. By the time my traveling companion turned around, I was several car lengths ahead.

Brock and Lawrence were waiting on the front porch by the time I arrived.

Lawrence stared at the following sedan as it drove by, then sped up. "I don't recognize that car."

"Rental?" Brock asked.

"Maybe." She turned to me. "How long did they follow you?"

"Two hours. It's like they had nothing else to do."

"Tell me what you were doing."

I took a deep breath in preparation for the eruption. "I went to talk to Robert Jenkins."

"Who is he?"

"Someone who used to work with my father."

"Let's go inside." She glanced up and down the street before following. Once inside, and the door closed and locked, she let loose with both barrels. "I told you I would look into questioning your father's former partners. But no, you go ahead, thinking you're invincible, and end up driving around for hours with a possible murderer on your tail."

"I thought they'd be more willing to talk to me out of respect for my father." I opened the back door and let Shutterbug out to do her business. "Asking questions isn't against the law."

"Impeding a police investigation is. All you're doing is making my job harder and increasing the risk to yourself." She unleashed her wrath on Brock. "If she doesn't have the sense God gave a goose, then maybe the two of you together might be able to have a full brain."

"Hey!" I glared. "Brock didn't know I was going. You can't yell at him."

"I can handle myself." Brock stepped forward. "We don't know that whatever happened in Kelly's father's day has anything to do with the deaths of Ben and Junior, do we?" He studied the detective's face. "But you think they do."

"I can't say."

"You wouldn't be this mad if they weren't connected," I said, idly patting Brutus's head as he jumped up and down to get my attention. "Shutterbug wasn't nervous in the slightest."

Lawrence rolled her eyes. "You're allowing a dog, albeit a good one, to dictate whether a situation is dangerous?"

"Yes." I crossed my arms. "She's a great judge of character."

"She isn't a police officer with a gun." Lawrence sighed. "A bullet can stop your dog."

"A bullet can stop anyone."

"I give up."

"I have to find out what got my father killed. I might not have started out with that as my motive, but it is now." I cleared my throat and leaned into Brock. "Somebody knows something and buried it to look as if his death was a random traffic-stop shooting. I don't think so anymore."

"I understand," Lawrence said. "Be careful. Your four-legged baby might not be able to keep you safe." Looking as if she carried the weight of LAPD on her shoulders, the detective climbed in her car and drove away.

"She's right." Brock turned me to face him. "We need to get our license to carry a weapon."

"That isn't what she said."

"Maybe not, but it's a good idea. That little pink canister of pepper spray can't be relied on."

"I know." I wasn't sure whether I could pull the trigger and shoot someone, though. Dad always said never to point a gun unless you planned on killing the person you aimed it at.

CHAPTER SIXTEEN

Brock insisted I do no more questioning of Dad's colleagues until I got my permit. Now, I had a pretty little 9-milimeter Ruger in the bottom of my already heavy camera bag and was on my way to see someone named Morgan after almost a week of delays.

I parked in the lot of an apartment complex on the edge of East LA. I'd brought the Volkswagen rather than the Corvette this time, but I was still glad I didn't have to go too far into gangsterville. In fact, I was surprised that an ex-cop would live so close to those he helped put behind bars.

The former officer lived in a corner apartment, first floor at the opposite end of the complex. Whistles and ribald comments followed as I passed open doors. Shutterbug would glance in their direction, effectively silencing the offenders. I smiled, very grateful for my faithful companion.

"Yoo hoo."

I turned to see Ruthie rushing toward me, Sassy's head bobbing over the top of her bag. "What are you doing?"

"Well, the more I thought about it," she put a hand to her heaving chest, "the less I liked you coming alone."

"I told Brock I was fine." He had wanted to cancel a dentist appointment in order to come with me.

"I've nothing else to do."

Sassy's yapping at everyone we passed was giving me a headache. "Tell her to hush or we'll anger Mr. Morgan before we get to talk to him."

"She's just saying hello, aren't you, my little sweet'ums?" Ruthie bent down so Sassy could lick her nose.

I exhaled into a groan and continued to Mr. Morgan's apartment. He leaned against the doorframe, a handsome man around Ruthie's age with salt-and-pepper hair, dark eyes, and a wide grin.

"I should have known this type of commotion could only come from Ruth Canyon."

Ruthie smiled and batted her lashes. "You aged very well."

I narrowed my eyes. "You knew who I was coming to see and that's why you followed me?"

She shrugged. "Maybe."

"Come on in." He might have invited both of us, but the way his gaze lingered on Ruthie led me to believe he'd forgotten I was there.

"Why here, Mark?" Ruthie surveyed the one-bedroom apartment. "Why this part of town?"

"I've got my reasons." He motioned for us to sit on a chocolate-colored leather sofa. He lowered his large frame into a matching recliner. "As I'm sure you have one for being here."

"This is Kevin's daughter." Ruthie grew serious. "She's the one with the questions." She let Sassy out of the bag, and the little ball of fur immediately jumped into Mr. Morgan's lap.

He stroked her coat. "You want to know about his death."

"Yes." I jerked, surprised. "Did Dixon call you and tell you I was coming?"

"No, but I've been expecting this day. I rode with your father when he was a rookie. We were partners until I made detective, then he followed a few years later and we became partners again. He was a good man."

"What was he digging into that got him killed?" I leaned my elbows on my knees and peered into his face.

"How did you find out about that?"

I explained about the case files and Junior's body behind the dumpster. Then I told him about Ben and the blackmails.

His gaze switched to Ruthie. "Someone is threatening you?"

"I received the demand letter yesterday." She pulled the envelope from her bag and handed it to him. "I'm to go sit on Huntington Beach, stare at the ocean with the money in a yellow bag next to me, and not turn around when the bag is taken."

"This says tomorrow. Have you told the police?"

"Why didn't you tell me?" I asked.

"I haven't decided what I'm going to do."

"This is bad. I'd started to think Junior Johnson was the blackmailer, but he's dead."

"Why would he have needed money, Kelly? His father is rolling in dough."

"What would the rich kid have to do with the dead maintenance man?" Morgan asked. "Think, Canyon. You're your father's daughter."

"They were seen coming out of a drug house minutes apart." I took my upper lip between my teeth. "The next thing we know, Ben was murdered. Then, we find the archived celebrity files in the drug house, which was set on fire with us inside. That links Ben and Junior, but they're both dead. I feel as if whatever Dad was working on is linked somehow, but can't find the link."

"Your father came to me shortly before his death. He was convinced one of our ten was involved in something illegal, and I'm not talking about stealing from the evidence room. This is bigger than that, and I doubt it's related to the death of Ben Jones. You have two mysteries here, Canyon."

I nodded. He might be right, but I needed proof. "What did my father tell you?"

"That one of the officers was taking hush money to cover up for a crime boss's activities. He was going to hand over what he'd found but was killed before he could. If you can find whatever he had, you'll have solved this case, at least."

"Who can I trust in the department today?"

"Lawrence. Don't trust anyone else."

"How do you know I can trust her?"

He grinned. "Because she's my baby sister. Her husband died of cancer a couple of years ago, and she's immersed herself in her career."

"Kelly is a burr under your sister's saddle," Ruthie said.

"I can imagine that. Lori doesn't like anyone stepping in what she considers her territory."

"Has she been here to talk to you?" I glanced up at the sound of the door closing. I hadn't heard it open, but there Lawrence stood.

"Not until now. Mark, how could you talk to a civilian about an open case?"

"Because her father meant a lot to me. Settle down, sis. I'll fill you in over dinner."

"You live here?" My eyes widened.

"No." Lawrence frowned. "This place is a dump. I think you're wrong, Mark. The murders are connected to whatever Detective Canyon was onto. I can't say more at this time. You'll have to trust me."

He glanced at her, then back at me. "I do. I also suggest you take advantage of this young woman's mind. She may not be law enforcement, but she's smarter than most of those bozos you work with."

Sassy jumped from Morgan's lap and squatted at Lawrence's feet. The detective jumped back, eyes wide in horror. "That little rat."

"Don't be mean to my darling." Ruthie scooped up the puppy. "It was nice seeing you again, Mark. Don't be a stranger."

"You either, Ruth. Still dancing?"

"How else do you think I stay in shape?" She

laughed and sashayed out the door.

Oh, horror. Morgan knew my grandmother during her stripper days. My face burned. "Yeah, I'll be in touch, too." I rushed outside, Morgan's laugh following.

"Grandma! You could have warned me that you knew him."

"Oh, those days are long gone, sweetie. I wasn't sure if he remembered me." A sly smile teased at her lips.

"You're quite unforgettable and don't forget embarrassing."

"Stop being a ninny. I'm not that person anymore, thank the Good Lord, and your father wasn't even a twinkle in his daddy's eyes. Lighten up." She climbed into the front passenger seat.

"How did you get here?"

"Uber."

"Oh. Now what?"

"We need to figure out what to do about my ransom note."

A tapping on the window drew our attention. A stony-faced Lawrence held the envelope we'd forgotten at Morgan's. I rolled down the window and reached for it.

"Nope." She held it high. "When were you planning on letting me know you'd received this?"

Ruthie leaned across me. "The very moment I decided what to do with it. I was going to burn it, but now that I have this sweet little Sassy, I don't want anything to happen to her. What do you recommend? Another trap?"

"I'll meet you at your house. Have Hanson be

there, too."

"She sure is one bossy woman," Ruthie said as we headed home.

I called Brock on the way home and he was there before us romping across the lawn with Brutus while passersby took pictures with their cell phones. I didn't think I'd ever get over wondering how he could ignore the fans and continue on as if nobody watched. "That man is very comfortable in his own skin."

"And what skin, huh?" Ruthie winked and got out of the car.

Heat rushed up my neck and settled on my face. Yeah, what skin. I got out of the car, retrieved Shutterbug from the back seat, and watched as the three dogs yapped and leaped around each other.

Brock turned my way and grinned. I hoped that smile of his never failed to make my heart skip a beat. "Hey, gorgeous."

"You must be looking in a mirror." I lifted my face for a kiss.

Still ignoring the gaping fans, he cupped my face in his hands and gave me a slow, lingering kiss that took my breath away and made my legs weak. When he pulled me away, I said, "What a greeting."

"There's more where that came from." He smiled and leaned his forehead against mine. "Let's pose for the gawkers."

With his arm around my waist, we smiled and waved before Brock whistled for the dogs to follow us into the house. Two of them came without a problem. Ruthie had to chase Sassy, who insisted on barking at the people on the sidewalk as if she were a rottweiler rather than a one-pound pup.

Laughing, I headed to the kitchen to make coffee while we waited for Detective Lawrence. My thoughts settled on Ruthie's demand letter. If my hunch was right, the police would want to again try and tempt the blackmailer by seeming to comply with his or her demands. I also figured it would be a hired someone that made the grab, just as it was on the Walk of Fame.

I poured water into the reservoir. What if something went wrong? This wasn't a woman I'd just met; this was the grandmother I loved. The only family I had left in the world.

"What's wrong?" Ruthie came up behind me, turned me around, and peered into my face.

"Just worried about your letter."

She put a hand on my shoulder. "Why? There's nothing you can do. Worrying won't change what the outcome will be. Faith, sweetie. I don't think God is ready for me yet. I've a lot of maturing to do before then."

I laughed. "That you do, Grandma."

"I'm resenting that word less and less." She gave me a hug. "Hurry with the coffee. Detective Lawrence is here, and you know how impatient she is. I put Sassy in her lap to keep her occupied. She didn't look happy."

"She doesn't strike me as a dog person." I pressed the button on the coffeemaker. Within seconds, the rich aroma of java filled the kitchen and eased the stress in my neck.

When I entered the living room with four mugs of coffee on Ruthie's favorite silver-plated tray, Lawrence was putting Sassy on the floor. I set the tray on the coffee table.

The detective glanced up. "Let's talk about Ruthie's demand letter."

"She got one?" Brock pulled the familiar envelope from his pocket, folded and tattered, but very recognizable. "So did I."

CHAPTER SEVENTEEN

"You're both supposed to have the money ready tonight? Both at Huntington?" I collapsed onto the sofa. "Do you have the money?"

They nodded in unison.

"Just in case," Ruthie said.

Lawrence's face darkened. "When were you going to tell me?"

"Tonight," Brock said. "I don't want the same thing to happen that happened with Olivia. Too many people. We can handle this."

"No, you can't." She whirled to face him, her nose mere inches from his. "None of you can. I'm calling the department for some undercover officers to stroll along the beach."

"We can't watch both of them at the same time." I shuddered. "They're going to be too far apart."

"You mean you can't watch both of them." She transferred her wrath on me. "The officers can. If you had any sense, you'd stay home out of the way." She marched into the kitchen, presumably to call for backup.

"I can handle myself, Kelly." Brock sat next to me and took my hands in his. "You keep an eye on Ruthie."

I nodded, knowing full well I'd be doing my best to run between them. "We have to catch this person, and it isn't going to be whoever snatches the bags. We've not heard from the one who hired Jason, so it's time to visit our friendly neighborhood Spider-Man again."

"Not going to happen," Lawrence said, returning to the living room. "He was found dead this morning. If not for his sideline of work, we'd have chalked his death up to a random act of violence."

"But not now," I said, the words catching in my throat.

"Not now." Lawrence set her lips firmly.

"This is not good at all." Ruthie nuzzled Sassy. "No, it isn't. We need to grab one of the bag snatchers tonight and make them talk, don't we, sweetie? Yes, we do. Whatever it takes." She rubbed noses with the pup.

The three of us stared at her as if she were crazy. Yes, we needed to do just that, but hearing it said in a squeaky baby voice made the situation surreal.

"Okay." Lawrence shook her head. "Let's get ready. Mrs. Canyon, you have the money in a red bag, correct? Hanson?"

"Paper sack."

"Really?" She frowned. "This perp does whatever he or she can to keep us off kilter." She glanced at her watch. "We have an hour. Time to go."

We loaded up, dogs and all, into a police van. I didn't think it a good idea to arrive in something so conspicuous, but Lawrence insisted the standard issue, black van wouldn't attract undue attention. Maybe not if it had a church or sport's team on the side. Instead, the plain sides seemed to blare "don't look at me."

The driver parked at the end of the parking lot as far from a street light as possible. We all climbed out the back of the van. Leaving Lawrence behind, we set off across the sand, Brock veering left as we neared the water's edge.

"Here, Ruthie." I motioned to a small sand hill, eyeing the Italian-made sandals on her feet. "Any closer and you'll get wet."

"Good point." She sat down, spreading the skirt of her sundress around her and removed her shoes. "In case I have to give chase."

"Riiight." I glanced to where Brock was little more than a silhouette, then sat next to Ruthie. I released the leash from Shutterbug's collar. "Go to Brock."

She whined, but when I waved my hand, raced away.

"Are you sure?" Ruthie put a hand on my leg.

"Yes. Brutus isn't old enough to do anything, and I've shed a lot of the fear that had a hold on me since Amber tried to kill me. Brock needs Shutterbug more than the two of us do."

"Don't forget Sassy."

I smiled. "Ferocious Sassy. I'm pretty sure the only thing she can protect us from is a seagull." I wrapped my arms around my knees and stared at the waves. The moon's rays tipped them with silver, creating a path I used to dream that led to heaven. Foolish teenage dreams.

As an adult, I knew the silver was an illusion and the inky darkness would suck me under to a place from which I could never return. I missed my father, but not enough to walk out into the water and never look back.

How was Dad's death connected to the recent murders? Lawrence had suspicions she kept from me, I knew it. That was her prerogative as a detective. But if I knew everything she did, was privy to the information in her head…

A man in a wet suit and snorkeling mask emerged from the water like a merman of death. Sassy darted up to him barking with all her might.

The man glanced down, picked the pup up by the scruff of her neck, and tossed her into the waves. Ruthie screamed and rushed into the water.

The snorkeler held up a knife, then motioned toward Ruthie. I froze. I understood his threat.

He pulled a large waterproof pouch from inside his suit, dumped the cash into it, then raced for the water's edge as Shutterbug dashed toward us. Three police officers, plus Detectives Lawrence and Sawyer sped toward us from the opposite direction. The masked man tossed us a wave and dove into the water.

"It's too late for here. Get over to Hanson,"

Lawrence barked to the officers. "Where are our undercover cops?"

I leaped to my feet and went to help a drenched Ruthie and shivering puppy from the water. "Is she okay?"

"She's just fine." Ruthie swiped the back of her hand across her eyes. "I've never been more frightened in my life. Wait until I find out who is behind this horror." She held Sassy tenderly to her chest and splashed her way to the sand.

I glanced back toward Brock just in time to see our merman emerge from the water. "Go, Shutterbug! Lawrence!" I pointed, then ran.

As we ran toward Brock, he stood. He and the other man grappled. One of them fell. Considering the one still standing grabbed the bag and shoved it into the one containing Ruthie's money. Brock was still down.

"Stop. Police." Lawrence aimed her pistol.

The merman saluted, then headed into the ocean, Shutterbug right behind him.

"Protect that dog," Lawrence ordered. "Go after them."

Hoping, praying they'd keep my dog from harm, I fell to my knees beside Brock. "Where are you hurt?"

He removed his hand from his side. The dark stain of blood coated his t-shirt. "I think I need stitches." His eyes rolled back and he fell backward.

"Brock. Help! We need an ambulance." I pulled off my t-shirt, not caring who saw me in my bra. It was more modest than most bathing suits. I pressed the shirt to the wound in Brock's side. "Stay with me, Brock. I've not had the chance to be your leading lady." Tears clogged my throat. "You foolish man. Why fight someone with a knife? It's only money."

"An ambulance is on its way," Lawrence said, standing over me.

Shutterbug's bark drew my attention back to the water. She latched onto the thief's arm, preventing him from going under the water. When the man raised the knife, Sawyer fired. The man fell backward, and Shutterbug released him.

Two officers splashed through the waves and retrieved the injured man.

"Good shooting," Lawrence said. "You only winged him. Now, we've got someone to question."

"Not until I do this." Ruthie yanked the man's mask as far from his face as it would go, then released it, snapping it against his nose and forehead. "That's for tossing my dog." With a shake of her head, she plopped onto the sand as the man cursed and the cops handcuffed him.

A nervous laugh escaped my lips. My grandmother never ceased to amaze me.

Shutterbug nudged my arm, then licked Brock's face. Brutus, who had cowered a few feet away, finally joined us and curled up against Brock's side.

"Don't worry, fella. You'll be big enough to help someday." Ruthie patted his head.

I kept pressure on Brock's wound, only moving aside when the paramedics arrived. They loaded him on a gurney and carried him across the sand to a waiting ambulance. "Ruthie, take care of Shutterbug. I'm riding with Brock."

"I'll make sure all three dogs are home safe," Lawrence promised, "then I'll join you at the hospital."

With a nod, I hurried after the paramedics.

Brock was stitched and given blood before he woke. I sat by his bed and stared at his pale, but still handsome face. "You silly man. You only play a hero in the movies where the bullets are blanks and the knives made of rubber."

He squeezed my hand before opening his eyes. "I want to be your hero."

"That you are." I placed a kiss on his forehead. "What were you thinking?"

"I didn't want him to get away. I didn't see the knife until it was too late. Did he get away?"

"No, he's in custody."

"I'll be questioning him later." Lawrence entered the room and approached the bed. "Actors."

Brock laughed. "Ouch. I think I recognize him from somewhere. I know I only saw his eyes and chin, but something about the man seems familiar."

"Think hard, Hanson. This could be the break we've been looking for."

"I'll focus on it when I'm not fuzzy from pain killers."

She gave an answering nod. "I'd like to purchase Shutterbug to be trained as a K9."

"Would that mean she would no longer be mine?"

"Yes."

"Then my answer is no."

"Her intelligence is wasted as a pet."

"She's my pet, my service dog, and my friend. If you want to use us as you did in the vacant lot with the police files, then I'm more than happy to oblige, but I will not sell her." I slipped my hand from Brock's as he fell asleep.

Lawrence seemed to think for a moment, then motioned her head toward the door. "Walk with me. I need coffee."

With a glance to make sure Brock was deeply asleep, I followed the detective into the hall. My steps faltered when I noticed the armed officer stationed outside his door. A second glance showed it to be Morgan.

"I thought it a necessary precaution. Now that we know Hanson may know the perp, it's more important."

"I thought your brother was retired."

"He is, but he hires out as security on occasion. He's the only one I can trust right now."

We entered the hospital cafeteria where Lawrence purchased two cups of coffee before leading me to a table in the corner. "I have to admit I'm stymied on this case, Canyon."

"Sawyer isn't much help?"

She stiffened, then shook her head. "I'm coasting pretty much alone on this one. The fewer people who know I'm following up on what your father started, the better."

Her voice had softened talking about Dad. I sat silent and blew into my coffee wondering how old Lawrence was. She looked to be about forty, but age could be deceiving. Ruthie was proof of that. "Did you know my father?"

She nodded.

"Were you an…item?"

She sighed and straightened. "Not openly, but yes, your father and I were seeing each other up until a few weeks before his death."

"You were at his funeral. You stood in the back."

"I did so out of respect. The department frowned on officers in romantic relationships. I was a rookie, he was a detective. I'd put in for a transfer but didn't receive one until after Kevin died."

"That's why you put up with me."

A sad smile crossed her face. "Pretty much. I can only tolerate so much, Canyon, but when you interfere with police business, you cross the line."

"You might as well call me Kelly." I stared at the dark liquid in my cup. "This is the worst coffee I've ever tasted."

"You've never had the department's coffee."

I laughed. "Did Ruthie know about you and Dad?"

"He said his mother knew he was seeing someone, but not who that someone was." Then, Lawrence did something completely unexpected. She reached across the table and squeezed my hand. "I loved your father dearly."

CHAPTER EIGHTEEN

I stood outside the locked storage building a few days later at the back of the studio and wondered how I could get inside without being discovered. We'd finished filming for the day, and since Ruthie was having dinner with Doug, and Brock was still working, I was here with my faithful companion. "I could climb through a window," I told her, "but you couldn't. With that padlock on the door, I couldn't let you in once I got inside. It's time to talk to Rod again."

"I'm here."

I shrieked and whirled. "You shouldn't sneak up on people."

"One of the cleaning gals told me someone was lurking around back here. I came to see." He grinned. "Why do you want in there? Nothing but old files."

"I really need to see for myself."

He pulled a large ring of keys from a clip on his

belt and unlocked the padlock, then pulled against the door. It opened with a loud screech. "See?" He waved his arm inside. "Nothing but boxes."

"Huh." I held out my hand and wiggled my fingers. "Flashlight?"

"Just hit the switch." He laughed. "You're way too cloak-and-dagger, young lady." He pressed a button on the wall.

The fluorescent light overhead was missing a few bulbs, but enough light remained to see that boxes filled the space. Still, I knew some were missing. I'd seen them with my own eyes. "How are these arranged? Alphabetical?"

"Yes." His brow furrowed. "What are you looking for?"

"I think a lot of the files have been stolen from here. Older actors. Where do they keep the non-archived files?"

"With their managers, I guess."

I needed to ask Brock who his agent was. "Who else has access to this building?"

"Just me and…Ben." Sadness clouded his face. "I reckon he would have let anyone inside that asked."

"Would he have let them remove files?"

"Only if they were entitled."

"Hmmm." I headed down the aisle of file boxes until I came to where Ruthie's should have been. Not there. Further exploration showed Olivia's was gone, too. "Does anyone keep a record of what's in here?"

"I'm sure they do. Why?"

"I know some are missing. I'd like to find out

exactly which ones."

"That would be quite a job."

"Not if I had help." I smiled. Fifteen minutes later, I was in the studio office waiting for the receptionist to print off the long list I'd need. While I waited, I asked Brock and Lisa to meet me at the storage building to help with promises of monetary payment for Lisa and a home-cooked meal for Brock. Both agreed.

Mr. Johnson entered the office and headed down the hall. I grabbed the list from the receptionist's hand and hurried after him.

"Mr. Johnson, may I have a word with you?"

He turned. "Make it quick. My son's funeral is today. I'm only here to pick up a few things."

"I am very sorry for your loss. Have they uncovered any information about your son's death?"

He narrowed his eyes. "Are you a reporter?"

"I wish. I'm an actress here. I'm starring in a series with—"

"Ruthie Canyon. Yes, I remember now. No, they haven't discovered anything new."

"Would Junior have been interested in blackmailing actors?"

He thought for a moment. "That's not appropriate, young lady."

"I'm sorry, sir. It's just that the person who killed your son shouldn't get away with it."

The anger left him, and with it his strong façade deflated like the air from a balloon. He shook his head. "You're right. To answer your question, yes, if it would bring him a quick buck, yes. I've withheld any allowance due to his drug habit. He might have done something like that to get money, but I doubt he'd be the brains behind the operation. Junior wasn't the brightest pebble on the beach." He sighed. "Don't get me wrong, Miss Canyon. I love my son, but he was a challenge."

"If he wasn't the brains, who would he have worked with?"

"Anyone who could get him what he wanted. Now, if you'll excuse me." He turned, entered a room, and closed the door before she could ask further questions.

That cemented in my mind that Junior and Ben had been working together. With both of them dead, there had to be a third. But who?

I sent Lawrence a text to search the bank accounts of her fellow officers. I was sure she'd already thought of it, but if one of them was in financial straits it might give us a step forward in the investigation. If the department still had a dirty cop in its midst.

Noting the time, I hurried back to the storage building where Rod stood outside with Brock and Lisa. He gave me a hand radio. "Call me when you're ready for me to lock up."

"Will do." I turned to Brock. "Are you feeling up to this?"

"I won't be doing anything but reading names, right?"

I nodded.

"Then, I'm fine. I've been told no heavy lifting because of the stitches. If I'm not doing any of that, then let's get going."

"Great." I divvied up the list. "Everything is alphabetical. Circle the name if they aren't here. It will give us an idea of who might be next on the blackmailer's list."

"Oh, this is fun." Lisa practically skipped into the building. "No need for payment. Excitement is all I need."

We hit separate areas of the building and worked in silence, checking names off our list as we found them and circling the ones we couldn't. After two hours, we had twenty names circled. Of that twenty, one was Doug, another one Louie. Our suspect didn't stick just to actors. The storage room seemed to contain all employee files.

"This is daunting," I said, leaning against the door.

"Hand it over to Lawrence and let her handle contacting them," Brock suggested. "Narrowing down the names will be a huge help to her."

"True, and I do need to see whether she'll let me in on her interview with the man who stabbed you."

"Somebody stabbed you?" Lisa's eyes widened. "How have I not heard about this?"

"We're trying to keep it out of the tabloids," I said. "Please keep it among us."

She crossed her heart and mimed locking her lips. "You can count on me."

I truly hoped so. I'd already trusted her with a lot considering the Internet search and now this. "I spoke with Mr. Johnson. Did you know Junior's funeral is today?"

"Yes." Lisa nodded, glancing at her cell phone. "In an hour, actually."

"Do you feel up to going?" I asked Brock. "Killers often show up at the funeral of their victims."

"Sure. Let's get changed out of jeans. We should make it in time. The first hour is the visitation with the memorial to follow."

Lisa jogged after us as we headed for the parking lot. "I'd like to go. I went to school with Junior."

I grinned. "Sure. I'm bound to have something that will fit you." I snapped my fingers for Shutterbug to come. Brock promised to meet us at the house in forty-five minutes. Not a lot of time to get ready, but a change of clothes, a quick brush of my hair, and it would have to do.

Ruthie seemed surprised to see Lisa, and also wanted to come along to the funeral. The three of us rushed to change, me tossing Lisa an eggplant-colored dress while I opted for navy. Ruthie went all out in black, complete with hat and veil.

"You look like his widow rather than someone who barely knew him," I said.

"Dramatics, dear." She smiled, kissed the nose of Sassy, and grabbed a bright red purse. "A girl must always have a pop of color."

A funeral wasn't the place for dogs, but it was still hard for me to close the door on Shutterbug's big eyes when Brock pulled into the driveway. "Let's take Ruthie's 1970 Aqua-colored Camaro." I jingled the keys. "She used to have a Stingray, but sold it years ago."

I didn't have to ask twice. Lisa scampered into the backseat like a kid going to a carnival. Brock sat up front with me, Ruthie in the back. I smiled and tossed Brock the keys. "You can drive."

"You mean it?" He jumped from the car. "Ow. No fast moves." He put a hand to his side. "I'm surprised she let anyone drive this car but you."

"I trust you, and she trusts me." I slid into the passenger seat while he hurried to the driver's side.

Once he was seated, he ran his hands over the steering wheel, then the dashboard.

"If you don't stop caressing the car," Ruthie said, "we're going to be late."

"Wow. A guy can't take time to revel in a gift." He inserted the key into the ignition. "I hope you ladies don't mind the top down, because it isn't going up." He pressed the accelerator.

"Yahoo!" Lisa surfed the air with her hand. "I've never felt this good on my way to a funeral before."

Brock took us the long way around. "Can't drive a convertible without the ocean breeze."

I laughed. "I should have let you drive a long time ago." I would have if I'd known it would make him this happy.

"Yes, you should have." He flashed me a grin. He turned off the highway and soon pulled into a Sonic. "I'm starving. We'll order and eat fast. No dropping food on the upholstery or Kelly will never let me drive again."

"What exactly are we looking for at this funeral?" Lisa asked, leaning crossed arms on the front seat. "I know you aren't going because you actually liked Junior. Few people did."

"Who might have killed him and Ben Jones." I

leaned across Brock and ordered popcorn chicken and a slurpee.

Once orders were placed, Brock shifted in his seat. "It isn't as if the killer will hold up his hand and say it's him."

"Or her. Remember Amber." I shuddered.

"How could I forget the scariest night of my life." He leaned over and kissed me. "No more running from crazy people without me."

Lisa sighed. "I wish I could find a man who'd face danger with me."

"I've been meaning to ask," Ruthie said. "Why don't you have a boyfriend? You're attractive enough."

"Me?" Lisa put a hand to her chest. "Frizzy haired, freckle-faced, brown-eyed Lisa Rogers? I look like Little Orphan Annie."

"Don't sell yourself short." Ruthie tapped her on the shoulder. "Put some care into your appearance and see what happens. Maybe be a little less…hyper."

"Ignore her," I said, shooting Ruthie a sharp look. "Don't be anyone but who you are."

"That's right," Brock added, paying the roller-skating waitress. "Kelly didn't have a stitch of makeup on and her hair was up in a ponytail the first time I laid eyes on her. I thought her the cutest thing I'd ever seen."

"How romantic." Lisa's lashes fluttered. "Maybe I just need to get out more."

I straightened. "Look. Louie's a few spots over. I didn't think he'd be caught dead in a fast food place."

"Considering he's wearing a suit, I bet he's headed to the same place we are." Ruthie lifted her veil for a better look.

Brock handed us each our order, then tapped the horn. He waved when Louie glanced over.
Louie frowned and turned his head away from us.

"That's rude." I frowned.

"He probably sees enough of us at work." Ruthie popped a piece of chicken into her mouth. "I've got the feeling he's not a big fan of yours."

"Me? What about you?"

"I've known him for years. Of course, he likes me."

I shook my head at her crazy logic. "I see no reason for him to have an issue with me. I'm at filming mostly on time, do my job to the best of my ability, and otherwise leave him alone."

"The key words there are mostly on time."

"You're late whenever I am!"

"Semantics." She pursed her lips around the straw in her diet soda. "I don't understand why you're getting so upset. So, what if he doesn't like you?"

"I want everyone to like me."

She shook her head. "Not going to happen as long as you stick your nose into other people's business."

Brock laughed. "She has you there. Let's go stick our noses somewhere they don't belong."

CHAPTER NINETEEN

The funeral home parking lot was packed. Seeing all the expensive vehicles made me doubly glad I'd brought the vintage Camaro, although I still preferred my impractical Corvette. It was all about keeping up appearances, after all.

Standing like bookends on each side of the double-front doors were Detectives Lawrence and Sawyer. Both wore dark suits and sunglasses. I couldn't help but think they looked like wannabe FBI agents.

"I need to talk to you," I whispered to Lawrence as I strolled by on Brock's arm.

"After the service," she replied in a soft voice.

We signed the guest book right inside the door. I quickly flipped pages, scanning names and wished I had the time and privacy to snap a few quick pictures with my cell phone. When I'd finished, Brock led us into a crowded room lined with padded chairs.

"Wow," Lisa breathed. "Everyone who is anyone is here."

Ruthie chuckled. "Everyone has to keep face with the boss, sweetie. I doubt Mr. Johnson will know, or care, but no one wants to take that chance." She sailed away to talk to Olivia.

"What do we do now?" Lisa asked.

"Keep your eyes and ears open for anyone acting suspicious."

She laughed. "In Hollywood? Everyone acts…different."

True. "Okay, different for here." I scanned the room, seeing several A-list stars and lots of B-list. I guess the upper echelon didn't care as much about schmoozing. I assumed the other expensively dressed people were upper-class acquaintances of the Johnson family.

Mr. and Mrs. Johnson stood next to a casket and shook hands as people filed past offering their condolences. I hung back as Brock inched forward.

"No thanks. After my father's funeral, I said I'd never look into a casket again. It's too creepy."

"Okay, babe. Wait here. I'll be right back."

Not likely considering the length of the line. Since I had some time without watchful eyes on me, but was safe enough with a crowd of people around me, I went in search of someone to talk to. I had no suspects. The only two I'd had were dead. A few people around me actually looked mournful, most simply bored, but one man, pale and sweating, drew me like a cat to a mouse.

He thought he was inconspicuous, half hidden behind a silk ficus tree, but it made him stand out to me. I skirted along the edge of the room and sneaked up behind him. Then I tapped him on the shoulder. "Excuse me."

He whirled, knocking over the tree. "What the heck, lady?"

"Hello." I smiled and righted the tree. "How did you know the deceased?"

He glowered. "Why do people always ask that at funerals? Does anyone really care?"

"Some do." I peered closer at his face, noting the dilated eyes. "Are you his dealer?"

"Shh." He grabbed my arm and dragged me into a nearby alcove. "Do you need something?"

I shook my head. "Just answers."

"Are you a cop?"

"No, an actress."

"Really? I don't recognize you."

"Yeah, I get that a lot." I crossed my arms. "Do you know how the drug house over near the Chinese theater burned down?"

"Fire?" He laughed at his own stupid joke.

"Seriously?"

"Someone paid me a hundred dollars to torch the place."

"Did you know people were inside?"

He staggered backward. "What? I killed someone?" He clutched his stomach.

"No, we got out."

"You were in there?"

I nodded. "Who paid you?"

"I don't know. A man came up to me, told me not to turn around, and slipped me a hundred-dollar bill. He told me what he wanted me to do, then left.

Setting fire to that old place was the easiest job I've ever had."

"Did you know there were boxes in one of the vacant rooms?" I glanced over to where Brock had noticed me gone, stepped out where he could see me, waved, then moved back to the alcove.

"Lady, I don't care what was in that building."

"Junior never said anything to you about files?"

"Nope. Look. I've paid my respects. Now, I've got to go before the cops find out I'm here. We aren't exactly good friends."

"I wouldn't imagine."

"I'll try to watch one of your movies. What's your name?"

"Kelly Canyon."

"The writer?"

My mouth fell open. "You read?"

"Why wouldn't I? Of course, I do. Especially true crime." He grinned, revealing the bad teeth of a meth addict. "Am I going to be in a book?"

"Most likely."

"All right!" He fist-pumped the air, then dashed across the room and out a side door.

Again, I'd learned nothing more but that the person responsible for the fire was a man, and our druggie arsonist. I probably shouldn't have let him go, but as Lawrence had told me plenty of times, I wasn't a police officer.

"I'm pretty sure we can stop calling our perp he or she and stick to he," I told Brock when he rejoined me. I filled him in on my conversation with Junior's dealer.

"What do you think Lawrence would say if she

knew you were talking to such a person?"

"She'd tell me it was dangerous. But how bad could it be surrounded by people?"

He opened his mouth to argue, then clamped it shut as everyone was asked to take their seats. I seized Brock's hand and dragged him as close behind Junior's family as we could get, which happened to be about the middle. Lisa had managed to coerce some poor young man into letting her sit next to him immediately behind Mrs. Johnson. The girl might make a good assistant after all. She was definitely daring.

I scanned the room for Ruthie, spotting her and Olivia sitting in the back with Doug. Hopefully, spread out as we were, one of us would hear something of importance.

The non-denominational pastor droned on about how God had picked a rose for his garden and how much Junior would be missed. I could be wrong, but not even Mrs. Johnson shed any tears as the pastor eulogized her son. What happened between a mother and her child that she wouldn't shed a tear at her son's funeral?

After the service, we were all invited to join together in remembrance of Junior in the adjoining banquet hall. Like sheep, we all trooped together. A large buffet table stretched along one wall while round tables filled the rest of the room. I never could understand the need to eat after the death of a loved one.

Lisa, Ruthie, and Olivia joined us at a table for four. Brock politely took a chair from another table and turned our table into one for five.

"Wait until you hear what I heard," Lisa whispered, leaning her elbows on the starched white tablecloth. "Wow." She ran her fingers over the cotton. "This looks more like a fancy dinner party than a memorial."

"Focus, Lisa." I stopped her hand. "What did you hear?"

"It turns out the man I sat next to," she waved across the room at the man, "is Junior's cousin. He told me that Junior had recently been disinherited and that he was next in line to inherit once the old man died." With a self-satisfied smirk, she crossed her arms and sat back in her chair. "That makes him a suspect, right?"

"Most definitely." I returned her smile. "What's his name?"

"Eric James Johnson, the third. Very aristocratic." She tilted her head to one side. "He seemed nice enough, though. Even a little embarrassed at being the next in line to inherit, but I've been around actors long enough to know not everyone is who they seem."

I watched the next richest man in Hollywood approach the buffet table. The slender, blond man who stood maybe five-foot-six didn't look like a killer. In fact, he seemed a bit shy by the way he avoided making eye contact with anyone and stepped humbly to the end of the food line. "Did he act as if he liked you, Lisa?"

"Well, he did let me sit next to him, and he blushed when I asked."

"Good. Go make friends with him. We need more information."

"But, he belongs to California elite. Why would he want to be friends with a makeup artist?"

"Sweetheart." Ruthie put her hand on Lisa's arm. "Smile but not like a shark, bat your eyelashes but not too much, and encourage him to talk about himself. Act helpless, but don't be."

"I'm confused," she said.

I rolled my eyes. "Just be yourself. Go."

"Okay. I can do this." She took a deep breath, stood, smoothed the skirt of her dress, and got in line behind Eric.

"I need to teach that poor girl how to get a man," Ruthie said.

"She's only fishing for information, not trying to get engaged."

Ruthie shrugged. "You never know what could happen."

"I will never understand women." Brock stood. "The things you worry about. I'm going to get in line. I'm starving. I'll bring you a plate, Kelly." As soon as he made a move for the line, women swamped him. Even at a funeral, he drew them like flies.

"You might want to get in line, Kelly," Olivia suggested. "You've got to protect your man."

"If he can be swayed by groupies, then he isn't my man."

Someone tapped me on the shoulder. I turned to see Lawrence.

"Come with me," she said.

I grabbed my purse containing the list and hurried after her. "I have a lot to—"

"Not here." She pushed open a side door and led

me to her car. "Inside."

With raised eyebrows, I did as she said.

She slid into the driver's seat, checked to make sure all the windows were rolled up and doors locked, then turned to me. "What do you have?"

"You're more nervous than I've ever seen you, Detective."

"That's because I feel as if I'm working this alone."

"I'm here."

"I'm surrounded by possible suspects every minute of every working day." She put both hands on the steering wheel. "The pressure is about to kill me."

"You aren't making any leeway on finding out who killed my father?" My heart sank.

"Nope." She glanced at me. "Let's focus on the recent murders and blackmail instead."

"Did you get any information out of snorkel man?"

"A little, but I can't divulge that information."

I sighed. "Fine. You can't fault me for asking." I pulled the list from my purse. "We compared the inventory of files in the storeroom to this list and found twenty boxes missing. We need to warn these people that they may be blackmailed next. What if some of them have already handed over the money?"

"That would be unfortunate. Once you succumb to a blackmailer's demands, they usually return for more. I've done some background work on your grandmother. We may have prevented her from having to fork over the money, but with her being a stripper back in her wild days, there is a lot the blackmailer can use against her."

"Why? That's all in the past. It isn't a secret." Still, I knew Ruthie would do almost anything to keep her past buried. "There's more." I told her what Lisa had discovered.

"That is news to me and a very strong motive for murder."

"For Junior, yes, but why Ben?"

"I think Ben simply knew something he shouldn't. He may have let our perp into the storage building, but from everything I can find out about the man, he wasn't a criminal. It looks as if he gave them access, got suspicious, did some snooping, and got killed." She sent me a sharp look. "Very much like you're doing now."

CHAPTER TWENTY

"**What do you mean** Doug is on the blackmail list?" Ruthie plopped onto the sofa and read the list again. "We need to warn him right now." She jumped back up and scampered around the room trying to catch Sassy, who clearly didn't want to be caught.

Shutterbug's ears stood at attention. I bet if she could talk, she'd be laughing and encouraging the puppy to run. Brutus was a bit more vocal and joined in the fun with leaps, bounds, and barks. Utter chaos had erupted, and I collapsed onto Brock in laughter.

"It's not funny." Ruthie's shrill voice caused Shutterbug to tilt her head. "Somebody help me, so we can go warn my Dougie."

"All right." Brock choked off a laugh and set me aside, so he could get up. He scooped Brutus up in one arm, the poor dog's legs dangling awkwardly. It wouldn't be much longer before he was too big for

Brock to carry. Once the gangly pup was under control, Brock dug a dog treat from his pocket and held it out to Sassy. The diminutive canine ran straight to him and danced around on her hind legs.

"Thank you, Brock, but don't give that to her. She only eats organic dog treats." Ruthie pulled a morsel from her purse and let Sassy eat it from the palm of her hand. "Now we can go."

Doug answered his front door dressed in a baggy t-shirt with a large hole under one arm and a pair of faded flannel lounge pants. "I wasn't expecting company."

"Oh, Dougie, you're in grave danger." Ruthie planted a kiss on his cheek that left a smear of scarlet-colored lipstick and brushed past him. "Have you received a black envelope with threats of blackmail?"

He frowned. "No. What's this about?"

"Sit down, dear." Ruthie took his hand and led him to a leather sofa. "Explain, Kelly."

"I will." Brock set Brutus on the floor and then perched on the edge of the coffee table. "Someone has taken files from the employee storage room at the studio. They are blackmailing the people in those files. So far, myself, Ruthie, and Olivia Rogers have been contacted. Your name is on the list of missing files."

"Oh." His round face paled. "Well, I have a stack of mail on the foyer table I haven't gone through. Maybe we should."

"I'll get it." I headed into the foyer and brought the wicker basket holding the stack of mail to Doug. I'd never been in his home before and had expected something…grander, I guess. He'd been manager to some of Hollywood's greats, yet he lived a very humble life. I liked him better for it.

Two black envelopes sat among the bills and junk mail. One was the standard wait for further instruction. The other was the demand letter.

"I was supposed to have paid up yesterday." Doug's eyes grew wide. "I've nothing for them to harm."

I begged to differ and glanced at my grandmother. "You have Ruthie."

He turned to her and grasped her hands. "You've got to go away. Far away from here until this is all solved. Go to London or Paris. Alaska, even. Anywhere but here." He held her hand to his cheek. "You're the most important thing in the world to me."

"Hush, darling. I'm not going anywhere." She slipped her hands free and cupped his face. "You are very important to me, too."

Uncomfortable with their intimacy, I motioned with my head for Brock to follow me from the room. In the hall, I asked, "We need to get ahold of Louie. Things could escalate very quickly from here."

"I agree. We need to let not only Louie know, but the other names on that list. I'm not sure how much Lawrence will tell them when she visits."

"The least she can get away with, I'm sure. Still, she needs to know that Doug's payment wasn't made and he or Ruthie could be in danger." I pulled my cell phone from my purse and dialed the detective's number.

"Yes, Kelly." Her voice sounded as if she carried the weight of the entire police force on her shoulders.

"We're over here at Doug Lincoln's house and he didn't check his mail for a couple of weeks. Anyway, he received the two letters. The drop date was yesterday. He didn't make it."

"Text me his address. I'm on my way."

"Detective? I'm afraid Ruthie may be in danger. She's the most important thing to him."

"I'll provide a bodyguard. How about Morgan?"

"Sure." That ought to be interesting with their prior relationship. Still, the man was the best thing we could get right now. I could only hope his being around Ruthie, after knowing her in the past, wouldn't interfere with the good thing she had going with Doug.

The four of us sat quietly, occasionally smiling at the antics of one of the dogs, until Shutterbug raced to the front door signaling someone's arrival. We glanced at each other, then Brock stood. "I'll get it."

"Be careful," I said.

"I will." He disappeared into the hall, calling out a second later that Detective Lawrence had arrived.

Exhaustion lined her face. "This case is going to kill me. Let me see the letters, please." She snapped on a pair of gloves. "I'm sure all of you have touched these."

"Actually not." I grinned. "Only Doug and the perp."

"Miracles are real." She read the letters. "Your protection will be waiting for you at your house,

Mrs. Canyon. My brother, Morgan Lawrence, will keep you safe until we find who is behind these threats."

Ruthie paled, but didn't say anything. "What about Doug?"

"I think it best if Mr. Lincoln stay at your place." She slipped the envelopes into a paper sack. "Miss Canyon, where are you headed next? Don't think I don't know you aren't planning to visit every name on that list."

"It will have to wait. I have filming tomorrow." Which gave me the perfect opportunity to warn Louie.

"Good night." She glanced at each of us in turn. "Keep your wits about you."

The next day, I did my best not to upset Louie. In fact, I was so pleasing and accommodating that he scowled at me most of the time. I didn't have the opportunity to talk to him until filming broke for lunch. As he headed for his office, I rushed to catch up with him.

"Louie, a minute, please."

"What? I'm hungry."

"We can talk over lunch. Let me have something delivered from the cafeteria and meet you in your office."

He stared at me for a minute. "You aren't going to get all weird and flirty like last year, are you?"

"No. I promise." That little episode of trying to get information out of him had resulted in nothing but embarrassment for us both.

I was promised two chicken salad sandwiches, fries, and coleslaw in fifteen minutes. Not exactly a low-carb lunch, but Louie didn't strike me as low carb. The man's middle got a bit rounder each year.

I'd ordered on my way to Louie's office. Shutterbug followed close behind. I knocked and entered.

"Does that dog go everywhere with you?"

"Yes." I grinned. "Don't you like dogs?"

He narrowed his eyes. "What do you want?"

I explained to him about the blackmail letters. "Did you get one?"

"Some files are missing?"

"Yes. Did you get a letter or not?" I sat in the chair opposite him. "This is important, Louie, and part of an ongoing police investigation."

"Yeah, I got two." He opened his desk drawer and dropped two envelopes on top. "I got them a week ago."

"Did you pay the money?"

"Of course, I paid the money. I can't have my ex-wife finding out everything I did while we were married. She'll take me to court and have the alimony raised. This is cheaper in the long run."

"They won't stop, Louie. You should have called the police."

A knock on the door announced the arrival of our lunch. I accepted the tray and set it on Louie's desk. As I turned, I spotted a stack of unopened mail. Sandwiched between two white envelopes was another black one.

"You got another one."

Louie bolted out of his chair and grabbed the black envelope. He ripped it open. "They want forty thousand this time." He ran his free hand through his hair. "I can't afford this if it's going to keep increasing." He whirled to face me. "If I don't pay, they'll hurt Maria."

Despite his cheating ways, Louie still loved his ex-wife. "We're trying to find out who is responsible. You cannot pay this." I urged him to sit back down. "Why don't you eat while I call the police. They'll keep Maria safe."

"How can I eat?"

"You can't help anyone if you don't keep up your strength." I dialed Lawrence's number. "You need to come to the studio. Louie's office."

She groaned. "On my way."

I pressed the off button and picked up my sandwich. "They'll be here soon. Cooperate, okay?"

He frowned. "Who do you think I am?"

"A very stubborn man who doesn't always listen to reason."

"Keep it up, Canyon, and I'll never have you in another film I direct."

I waved off his threat. "You're the one who got me started acting in the first place. I only act it because I like the money."

A laugh burst from him. "You're the only actress I know who isn't out for fame."

I shrugged. "I want to be a—"

"Photojournalist, I know. Everyone knows. I hear that you take dog photos now. Isn't that a step in the wrong direction?" He took a large bite out of his sandwich.

"It's good money."

"What's with you and money?"

"I want a lot of it. I want me and mine to be forever secure." I forked some of my slaw but didn't eat it. Instead, I let it fall back into the bowl. "I've always felt I needed to have a comfortable bank account…just in case."

"Sickness."

"I guess it really boils down to having enough stashed away that I can travel the world, looking for stories without worrying about how I'm going to pay my bills."

Detective Lawrence cleared her voice. "Did you receive a letter, Mr. Stock?"

"He received more than one," I said. "Isn't it ironic how you told me not to mention Ruthie's letter to anyone, yet half of Hollywood is receiving them?"

"Not half." She kept her focus on Louie's desk where all three envelopes rested. She frowned. "You paid the money?"

"Yeah, but now it has doubled." He slid the envelopes across the desk. "I need protection for my ex-wife."

"We'll keep an eye on her if she has nowhere she can go. Family out of the state? Perhaps a long vacation?" Lawrence slid the evidence into a bag.

"I'll ask her." Louie swiped his lunch off his plate and into the trash. "Not hungry."

"I need to know when you receive the next demand letter, Mr. Stock. Do not, and I emphasize, do not, pay the money. We cannot catch this man if you are accommodating."

"Okay. I'll call you or tell Canyon here. She always seems to be underfoot."

"Why, I didn't know you noticed." I stood and followed Lawrence from his office. "The blackmailer is twenty-thousand dollars richer."

If looks could sear, a hole would grace the wall of Louie's office. Lawrence shook her head. "Why are people so adverse to calling the authorities for help?"

We turned as a runner, one of the young people on the lot responsible for running here and there to do the bidding of the cast and crew, approached at a fast clip. "This came for you, Miss Canyon. It looked important, so I came to find you."

"Thank you." The deep red envelope chilled my blood more than the black one. I knew without opening it that the blackmailer had contacted me.

CHAPTER TWENTY-ONE

With trembling fingers, I opened it and read, "Forget money. I want the nose you keep sticking into my business." I handed it to Lawrence. "That sounds like a death threat."

"I agree." She punched a number into her phone. "ETA to Canyon house? Great." She hung up. "My brother is on his way. Do not go anywhere without him."

"I won't. I can promise that." I put a hand on Shutterbug's head to calm my nerves and concentrated on breathing. In…out…in… "I want Brock staying at the house, too."

"You'll be full, but I agree." She escorted me to my car. "Straight home, Kelly. Windows up, doors locked."

I nodded and drove home doing my best not to panic. Why would I receive a threat? I was nowhere near identifying the blackmailer. I kept an eye on my rearview mirror, relieved no one tried to run me off the road on my way home. I pulled into the three-car garage and closed the door before getting out of my car.

Morgan met me at the door. "Smart thinking." He nodded at the closed garage door.

"Being chased by a killer teaches a person things." I stepped into the kitchen. "Brock isn't here?"

"He's on his way," Ruthie said, setting a chocolate cake in the center of the table.

Doug's face brightened. "My sweetheart does know how to make a day better."

If only cake could force the blackmailer off our backs. "We never had the chance to warn the other names on the list."

"We can call them," Ruthie said. "It's not as personal, and they might hang up on you, but it's worth a shot."

"Or have Lori contact them." Morgan turned a chair around and straddled it. "That is her job."

I glanced from him to Ruthie. I'd expected tension with Doug in the room considering Ruthie's past, but the three seemed friendly enough. My grandmother most likely told Doug all about her past, filling in what he may not have known. Truth left no power in the hands of the wicked.

The sound of a key in the front door signaled Brock's arrival. I jumped up to greet him, only to be motioned back into my seat by Morgan. "I'll get the door."

Moments later, he returned with Brock, who set his worn duffel bag on the floor. "This looks like a rather somber party considering there's cake." He bent down and gave me a kiss, then leaned his forehead against mine. "Are you okay?"

"I'm fine. Receiving the threat had rattled me for a bit, but I'm good now."

"I hope this doesn't mean Louie will have to delay filming," Ruthie said. "He won't take that news well."

"I'll accompany you to the studio." Morgan resumed his seat and reached for a slice of cake. "Got milk?"

"Almond milk," Ruthie said.

Morgan visibly shuddered. "I'll be ordering groceries if I have to stay here longer than…an hour."

Laughter rang around the table. "Morgan has the front guestroom, Brock, so let me show you where you'll be sleeping."

He grabbed his duffel bag and followed me to the other end of the house. Glancing inside the ruffle-filled room, he said, "At least it's blue."

"Ruthie sometimes goes overboard with the feminine touches. Poor Morgan's room is predominantly yellow." I leaned against the doorframe. "I'm sorry you're being uprooted like this."

He gave a crooked grin. "Don't be. I get to be under the same roof as you for twenty-four-seven."

I smiled. "You might get tired of me."

"Never." He wrapped an arm around my waist and pulled me close. "Now, Ruthie…she might start to make some nerves twang."

"You'll get used to her. Just don't look at or talk to her until she's had her coffee and put makeup on.

If you do, you're taking your life in your own hands."

"I'll remember that," he whispered, his lips a mere breath from mine.

Someone cleared their throat.

I sighed and turned to Morgan. "What?"

"Lori is here to talk with all of you."

I glanced at Brock and shrugged. "She didn't say anything about coming over."

We followed Morgan to the kitchen where Lawrence and Sawyer had joined the crowd. A clear plastic bag containing individual smaller ones of black envelopes and a red one sat in the middle of the table.

"I've tracked down the supplier of these type of envelopes," Lawrence said.

"Hello to you, too." I sat down.

She exhaled heavily. "No time for pleasantries. These envelopes came from a low-budget wedding invitation printer. We're checking purchase receipts now, but I'm not holding out much hope in identifying who bought these. Red and black are fairly common colors. As for the list of names, I have officers visiting each name as we speak."

"You made a trip here to tell us something you could have done over the phone?" I crossed my arms.

Her gaze flicked to Sawyer. If I hadn't been studying Lawrence's face, I'd have missed it. "The chief is starting to get on our case about how long this is taking. Hollywood doesn't like to wait for anything."

"Especially when lives are at stake," Morgan

said. "Celebrities or not, your job is to protect and serve."

She frowned. "Thank you for the reminder."

"Just keeping your feet on the ground."

Her lip curled. "Miss Canyon, a word alone, please." She pivoted and slid between the French doors, keeping her back to the others.

I joined her. "What's wrong? Am I mistaken, or did you give a certain type of look earlier."

"I gave a look." She kept her voice low. "Don't say anything. Just listen. I don't want anyone reading your lips."

"I thought we could trust everyone inside." My throat seized.

"I don't think so. If I'm right, one of those people is the blackmailer."

"But everyone inside received a letter except for Morgan and Sawyer."

"I think the suspect sent himself one."

"Oh, you mean…"

She put a hand to her lips. "No talking."

She meant Doug. My legs threatened to give way. Ruthie would be devastated. I shook my head. It didn't make sense. Why would a successful acting manager resort to blackmail? I bowed my head. "He's living under my roof."

"Lock your bedroom door at night. Keep Shutterbug close to you."

Keeping my head down, I asked, "Why do you suspect him?"

"There is a video of him purchasing a box of black envelopes."

I sagged into a lawn chair as Brock burst onto

the patio. "What's going on? Kelly?"

"I'll keep you informed, Miss Canyon. Remember what I said." Lawrence went back into the house, closing the door behind her.

Brock knelt in front of me. "Talk to me, Kelly."

"She thinks Doug is the one blackmailing everyone."

"No!"

I nodded. "We need to get Lisa to do some background checking on him. She's a whiz on the Internet."

"Isn't Lawrence already doing that?"

"I'm sure she is, but if he is the one responsible, I want to know now so we can get him out of our house. He just doesn't seem like a killer to me."

"Money is a powerful influencer." He took my hand and pulled me to my feet.

The detectives were gone when we joined the others. I retrieved my cell phone from where I'd set it on the counter and texted Lisa. She replied back that she would get started immediately. I deleted our conversation and slipped my phone into the pocket of my baggy cotton slacks.

Nausea rose in my stomach as I watched Doug play lover to my grandmother. They laughed and whispered together. She'd be heartbroken.

Morgan also watched them with sadness in his eyes. Maybe with Doug out of the picture, Ruthie would turn to the handsome ex-cop for comfort. Morgan caught me looking and crooked an eyebrow.

I managed a weak smile and resumed my seat.

"What did Lawrence want?" Ruthie asked.

I jerked. "She was, uh, worried about me." I was an actress for crying out loud. Surely, I could lie without stuttering. "I didn't take the threat well at the studio."

"Why should she care that much?" Ruthie's gaze sharpened. "Unless you're keeping something from us."

"Did you know Dad had a female friend before he died?"

She nodded. "I'd never met her, though."

"It was Lawrence. She's trying to solve his death."

Ruthie clutched the neckline of her blouse. "Lawrence. Well."

"Anyway, we're comparing notes on what we find out about how Dad died." There. I'd told the truth for the most part. "Did you know, Morgan?"

"I suspected, but she denied it the one time I asked, and I let the matter drop. My sister's love life is her business, but I remember her being quite devastated when he died. I thought it was because they were once partners."

"I guess solving his murder is going to have to take a back seat to this blackmailing case." I fought the urge to glare at Doug.

Ruthie sniffed and got up from the table. She planted her hands flat on the counter and bowed her head. "I had hoped his death really was a random act of violence. Hearing it might be murder brings it all back home to stab me in the heart again."

Doug moved to her side, making me want to gag. I must have made a sound of disgust because Morgan shot me a questioning look. He motioned his head toward the living room and left, clearly expecting me to follow.

"We can't talk here," I whispered.

"What did Lori tell you out there." He pulled me to the furthest corner of the large room.

"She suspects Doug to be the blackmailer."

His eyes widened. "And he's sweet-talking Ruth. Don't worry, Kelly, I'll keep an eye on him."

"We need to find out his motive for killing Ben and Junior."

"If there is one, Lori will find it."

I nodded and plopped onto the sofa, breaking one of Ruthie's cardinal rules by letting Shutterbug on the sofa. Sassy immediately joined us. Brutus came from behind an armchair with one of Ruthie's Italian pumps in his mouth. "Oh, you're going to get it now, you rascal." I reached for the shoe only to have him dart away.

I leaned my head back, remembering the last time a puppy had a shoe in its mouth. It had been Shutterbug with a red paint-splattered gym shoe. Finding that shoe had been the first step in solving a murder. I doubted we would get that lucky this time.

"Was that my shoe in that beast's mouth?" Ruthie planted her fists on her hips. "Brock!"

"I'll get it." He rushed after the puppy. From the sounds coming from Ruthie's bedroom, a twister had touched down. Finally, Brock joined us. The pump sported very clear teeth marks in the leather. "I'll replace them. I promise."

Tears welled in Ruthie's eyes. "They're just a pair of shoes."

"Then what's wrong?" I hurried to her side.

"Life is a bit out of control. Sometimes, I need a good cry to put things back into perspective." She took the shoe out of Brock's hand and headed to her bedroom. The door closed with a click.

"She forgot to take Sassy." I glanced at Brock. "This isn't good. How is she going to cope when the truth comes out?"

Wait. Lawrence had given the look at Sawyer. Did she suspect him to be in cahoots with Doug? She had to believe she didn't have enough evidence or she'd have taken one or both of them away in handcuffs.

CHAPTER TWENTY-TWO

What was I missing? Later that night, I shut myself away in the dark room and studied my most recent photos I'd taken under a magnifying glass.

I saw nothing new in the photos of Ben and Junior leaving the infamous drug house. I moved to the poodle photos and enlarged the eyes peering from the hydrangeas. They could be either Doug's or Sawyer's. I moved the magnifier around the photo. There. Dark shoes. Something I'd missed earlier. Setting the magnifier down, I straightened to ease the kink in my back. I'd been poring over photos for hours. All I'd found were shoes. It always came down to shoes. Wait.

I hurried to Brock's room and knocked. "Are you awake?"

A drowsy Brock in cotton lounge pants answered the door. I swallowed hard and pulled my gaze away from his chiseled torso. Oblivious to my mouth-wide-open stare, Brock pulled his pants higher on his hips. "I am now. What's up?"

"Please tell me you took a picture of the footprints behind Olivia's bushes with your cell phone."

A sexy grin stretched his lips. "I did. I forgot all about it after Sawyer snuck up on us. Come in." He left the door wide open and flipped through the gallery on his phone. "Here."

A very distinct pattern of evenly-spaced squares were pressed into the soil. "Bingo. We're looking for dark shoes with this pattern. Find those and we find our killer."

He put an arm around my shoulders and squeezed. "You're the smartest person I know."

I cleared my throat and put space between us. It wouldn't do to stay around a sleepy, half-dressed Brock for very long. "Good night."

"Good night," he said huskily.

My heart raced, and I hurried from the room, closing his door behind me. I leaned against the raised paneled wood and closed my eyes. Idiot. You could have waited until morning to check if he'd taken the photo. I'd become too comfortable around Brock and that would never do. After that miserable time when I came close to marrying an abusive drunk, I vowed to never step over the intimacy line again and to take things slow.

"Well, well, little Miss Kelly." Morgan leaned against the wall.

"It's not what you think." I pushed past him.

"It's none of my business what two consenting adults do."

"We're looking for someone with dark shoes that have a distinctive square pattern on the sole."

He blinked. "What?"

"That's what Brock and I were doing. Studying photos." I reached for the handle on my bedroom door. "So get your mind out of the gutter and back on the case." I stepped into my room and slammed the door for emphasis.

I was the last one down for breakfast the next morning and took the empty seat next to Doug, my smile probably resembling a shark's grin.

His eyes widened. "Uh, good morning."

"Good morning." My gaze flicked to his shoes. Drat. Gym shoes, the type you'd wear to go running. No worries. I'd find a way into his closet. Here and at his home. Sawyer might be a bit trickier.

I pulled my cell phone from my pocket and sent a text to Lawrence about the shoes. Maybe she could check her partner's footwear. I set my phone on the table and helped Ruthie dis up enough scrambled eggs and bacon to feed an army.

When I turned to carry platters of eggs to the table, I noticed Doug straighten, his eyes darting away from the text messages on my phones. When I glared at him, he acting as if he hadn't been looking and focused on his coffee instead.

"Can I help you, Doug?" My voice could have frozen butter.

"No, but your phone buzzed."

I made a sound in my throat. After setting the platters on the table, I looked at the message from Lawrence. "I'm on it." I glanced up to see Doug's cold gaze settle on me.

Ruthie served his bacon and eggs, and he transferred his attention to her. He whispered something that made her blush and giggle, then with one more hard glance at me shoveled food into his mouth.

Yep. Mr. Chubby Doug Lincoln was not the friendly, carefree man he pretended to be.

"Stop," Morgan whispered. "You'll tip him off."

"He's sweet-talking my grandmother," I hissed.

"What's with all the secrets?" Ruthie frowned at me. "You're acting very strange, Kelly."

"I didn't sleep well." I ducked my head and pretended to be ravenous.

"You need to relax. I'll schedule us a massage for this afternoon. My girl will come to us."

I smiled, knowing I'd do whatever it took to keep my grandmother safe. "We'd better get a move on if we're going to get to the set on time."

Morgan pushed back his chair and stood. "Everyone goes, no exceptions. Mr. Lincoln, you'll do business from the set. Mr. Hanson, you go straight to your set and then back to us. No detours. Everyone nod if you understand."

We all nodded in unison. Five minutes later, chairs scraped the floor and the sound of footsteps heading to bedrooms filled the house. I shoved Shutterbug's leash into my camera bag/purse. As well trained as she was, she wouldn't leave my side unless I told her to. Still, leashes were required on the lot and I'd need one if someone complained.

"Heavens, girl," Lisa said as I sat in the makeup

chair half an hour later. "It's going to take some work to get rid of those bags under your eyes." She glanced at the sofa where Ruthie sat next to Doug. "Her skin looks smoother than yours today." She bent closer to my ear. "You need to find a way to ditch those two. I unearthed some interesting things buried on the Internet."

"Have lunch with me. We can't leave Morgan's sight, but we should be able to talk." I glanced to where Doug watched us, a suspicious look in his eyes. If I had doubted his guilt before, each murderous glimpse convinced me that he was our blackmailer and quite possibly a cold-blooded killer.

When we broke for lunch, Lisa and I filled our plates with fruit and finger sandwiches from the provided buffet and found a secluded corner where Morgan could still see us, but no one could overhear our conversation or approach us without our knowledge.

"Spill it, Lisa." I bit into a slice of honeydew melon.

"It wasn't easy. On the outside, Doug Lincoln is squeaky clean, but when you dig down and find out that his real name is Donald Lakin, well…" She wiggled her eyebrows.

"How did you find that out?"

"When I couldn't find any dirt on the guy, I decided to take a close look at his deceased wife. Ex-wife," she corrected herself. "Anyway, the marriage license read Donald Lakin. So, I did a bit more searching and found a photo. No mistake that they are one and the same guy. Now, Dougie Poo legally changed his name and manages actors under Lincoln. No crime there. Here's the juicy part…Donald had a gambling problem and racked up a lot of debt. Lauren paid that off with her acting. My guess is that Doug never got over that particular addiction and thinks that blackmail is a fast and easy way to make a quick buck." She grinned. "Confused yet?"

"I managed to keep up." I sat back in my chair. "That would explain his access to the files, but why kill Ben and Junior?"

She shrugged. "Ben knew too much."

I nodded. "Maybe Junior wasn't the rat in this scenario. Maybe he stumbled across the files in the drug house. I still can't see Doug murdering someone, though, but I didn't think Amber could either, and she was as crazy as a man talking to a Wilson volleyball."

"Now what?"

"I tell Lawrence what I've discovered and find a way to break the bad news to Ruthie." My heart fell. "She really likes the man."

"Better she find out now rather than later. Rumor has it that he's going to propose." Lisa leaned her elbows on the table. "Then he'll have access to her money. Just like he had with Lauren."

I couldn't let that happen. I texted Lawrence to meet me at the lot after filming. She arrived ten minutes later and watched the scene we were working on.

"I was watching over your Mr. Handsome," she said. "The man assigned the task today went to the hospital for the birth of his son."

"And you don't trust Sawyer."

"Correct, and no, I haven't had a chance to check out his shoes."

I told her what Lisa had dug up on Doug. Instead of being happy about the information, she scowled. "You're involving too many people."

"I'm no good on a computer and she is."

"You aren't a police officer."

I groaned. "You're welcome. Maybe you should hire Lisa to work for you."

"And have her get fired because she told you confidential information? No thanks." A smile teased at her lips. "But this is excellent information and puts another nail in Mr. Lincoln's coffin, so to speak."

"I think he suspects I'm on to him. He saw our text messages on my phone at breakfast."

She rolled her eyes. "Are you serious? Well, maybe this will draw him out of the woodwork. I've warned the others on the list not to give any money to the blackmailer. They've all agreed. If our hunch about Mr. Lincoln is right, he'll grow desperate and try something else."

"I heard he's going to propose to my grandmother."

"Proposing is one thing. Marriage another. He'll be locked up before they can say their vows. I promise you that." She shot a glance to where Doug sat reading a script. "You'd think with as many actors as he represents, he'd have plenty of money."

She sighed. "High stakes gambling will bring you down every time. Let me know if you find out anything else and stay close to Morgan." She patted Shutterbug's head before leaving.

Brock took Lawrence's place and gave me a welcoming kiss. "I have a feeling you have some things to tell me."

"Oh, boy, do I!" We cuddled on a loveseat while I filled him in. "We're getting close to the end, Brock. I can feel it. I need to get into his house to look at his shoes."

"I'll come to your room tonight around eleven. We can sneak out your window."

"Morgan already thinks we're…you know. He caught me leaving your room last night. Besides, I can't take Shutterbug out the window and she's the best warning system we could have. We'll have to slip out the back gate."

"Okay. How do you want to distract our guard dog?"

"That's the hard part. The man's like a ghost the way he flits around the house."

"There is no way the two of you can get out of the house without me knowing."

I glanced over my shoulder to see a stern-faced Morgan, muscled arms crossed, staring down at us. "Then come with us."

"And leave Ruthie home alone with a possible monster? Not a chance. I'll have Lori run by and check out the man's shoes. The two of you are staying where I can keep an eye on you. If someone kills Canyon's daughter, Lori will shoot me in the head."

CHAPTER TWENTY-THREE

"I'm going for a run," I called out as I headed for the front door with Shutterbug and Brock.

Morgan planted himself in front of us. "Nope. I'm pretty sure you aren't a runner unless zombies are chasing you. Even then you couldn't go unless we all go, and I can't see Doug going for a run. How about it, Doug?"

"Not my thing." The man barely looked up from the book he was reading.

I narrowed my eyes at the large man in front of me and hissed, "We need to investigate."

"I said to let Lori handle it," he said in a low rebuke that precluded any further argument.

"I'm going to get fat staying around here."

"Don't listen to her, Morgan," Ruthie said. "Kelly has a high metabolism."

Whose side was she on? Acting very much like a petulant child, I stormed to my room, slammed the door closed, and threw open the window. I could escape that way, but wouldn't be able to take Shutterbug. That thought alone made me hesitate.

"Sorry, girl." I scampered out before arousing Morgan's suspicions.

"Boo."

I clapped a hand over my mouth to stifle a shriek, then punched Brock in the arm. "You scared me half to death."

Laughing, he grabbed my hand. "Come on. We'll take my car. It's easier to reach since it isn't in the garage."

Feeling like teenage lovers sneaking out for a date, I hurried into the passenger seat of Brock's new Jaguar. "When did you get this?"

"Last week. I just picked it up yesterday. Had some personal details done."

"Gorgeous." Not only the car, but the grinning man in the driver's seat.

He put the car in neutral, then leaving his driver side door open, used his leg to push us away from the house before pressing the ignition button. Then, after giving me a high-five, we sped toward Doug's house.

"Lawrence is going to kill us," I said.

"If there's anything left of us after Morgan gets through."

"True. But if we can prove Doug is the killer, then maybe they'll kill us without too much pain." We shouldn't make light of the situation. Lawrence may have loved my father, but she'd also threatened many times to arrest me. This might be the very time she makes good on that threat.

Doug lived in a sprawling ranch house in an very upscale community. No wonder the man needed more money. If he had a gambling problem along with the upkeep on the five-thousand-foot house, he'd need a lot of cash.

A locked iron gate prevented us from going any further. Brock turned off the car's engine. "Let's find a way over the wall."

"Good thing we didn't bring Shutterbug after all." We squeezed through some oleander bushes.

"I'll boost you up," Brock said. "I can scale it." He cupped his hands.

I planted my feet, and with a grunt, he hoisted me to the top. I stopped, dangled my legs over until I determined there were no guard dogs to tear me apart, then dropped to an overgrown lawn.

Seconds later, Brock dropped with a thud beside me. "Let's find a way in." He pulled two small flashlights from his pocket and handed me one. "Always prepared." He tossed a wink my way and took off at a fast pace for the house.

I followed. We didn't have much time. Once Morgan discovered us gone, he'd call his sister and she'd show up to run us off or throw us in jail.

We found an unlocked back bedroom window and climbed into a sparsely furnished house. Considering the odd assortment of appliances, ones you could buy at Wal-Mart, Doug must have sold things to raise money. Especially since only one person had paid the demanded twenty-thousand dollars that I knew of, anyway. The only room not half empty was the office.

Papers, chairs, pens and pencils littered the floor

and every other available surface. "Bingo. If there's anything to be found, it'll be in this room," Brock said. "Except the shoes. You check the bedroom and I'll get started in this mess."

Flashlight firmly in hand, and providing just enough light to see ahead, I headed down a short hall and came to a master bedroom, separated from the other bedrooms at the opposite end of the house. A bed, a dresser drawer, and two nightstands hardly filled the cavernous room. And attached to a bathroom larger than most studio apartments was a large walk-in closet.

Doug didn't seem to have sold anything in there. Shoes filled one wall and clothes were jammed on clothing rods. This wouldn't be a fast task. Risking discovery, I closed the closet door and turned on the light.

I had planned to focus on dark dress shoes. The problem…all the dress shoes were in various shades of black and dark brown. How many of the same color shoe did one person need? With a sigh, I started flipping shoes over and looking at the soles. I checked every single pair and failed to find the ones I was searching for.

Standing in the center of the closet, I turned in a slow circle to look for shoes that hadn't been put away. Okay, if I were trying to get away with murder and had to leave temporarily, where might I stash?

The hamper.

I peered inside the dark leather container. Not readily seeing what I sought, I lifted the few shirts on top. Ta da. I pulled out a pair of black shoes with the incriminating pattern on the sole. We now had proof Doug was the man peering at us from the bushes. Now, to link him to the murders.

"Kelly!"

I hurried to the office where Brock stood in the center of the room clutching several sheets of paper. "What did you find? Here are the shoes." I set them on the desk.

"Bank statements. Doug was definitely struggling financially."

"Anything to link him to murder?"

Brock's shoulders slumped. "Lawrence has good reason not to trust anyone at the department. Doug paid Detective Sawyer five-thousand of the twenty-thousand he received from Louie."

"That doesn't seem like a lot to pay someone to commit murder."

"I didn't think so either." He opened a cabinet. "Here is the box of black envelopes and one single red one. In the printer tray is a typed letter to Detective Sawyer urging him to back off for a while until things cooled down. Doug said he had another way of making money, but it would take longer, then he would pay for an accident to happen." Brock's brow furrowed. "This sounds like he's trying to set the detective up. Why leave a note in the printer? It doesn't make sense."

I gasped. "He plans on killing Ruthie after he marries her. Of course he wants to take suspicion off himself."

"That's what I think, but I don't think the detective is an innocent bystander either."

"Aren't you two the smartest, dumbest, people I

know." Lawrence stood in the doorway. "Morgan called me once he realized you had climbed out your bedroom window. What were the two of you thinking?"

"That you needed help solving the case since you couldn't trust your partner. Am I right?" I tilted my head, then froze as someone stepped up behind the detective.

"I have to agree with Lawrence," Sawyer said. "The two of you are quite clever."

Lawrence went for her gun and aimed it at Sawyer.

Sawyer pointed his at his partner.

I picked up the closest thing at hand and threw it. The glass paperweight with a scorpion forever preserved inside barely missed Sawyer's head. He jerked and fired the gun.

Lawrence got off one shot before she fell.

Red blossomed across Sawyer's chest before he crumbled to the floor.

"Lori." I knelt beside her and felt for a pulse. "She's alive. We've got to get help."

"No, Kelly. You've got to get to Ruthie." Brock pulled me away. "I'll call an ambulance and see to the two of them. Go." He thrust his car keys into my hand. "Be safe." He planted a quick kiss on my lips, then gave me a gentle shove.

I whirled and dashed from the house. I'd been worried about how I'd get over the wall, but the iron gate sat open, thanks to the detectives. The new problem was the fact that the squad car blocked the Jaguar.

How much trouble could I get into if I were to

borrow the squad car? Was it worth saving my grandmother? Yes. I climbed into the driver's seat and felt for hidden keys under the seat. Bingo. I roared away. Sirens wailed in the distance.

Nobody got anywhere fast in Los Angeles traffic, and Doug had lived further from the studio than we did. Tonight, traffic seemed bent on preventing me from getting home. Traffic slowed to a crawl as we passed an accident. As I tapped impatiently on the steering wheel, I remembered leaving the shoes back at Doug's place and hoped Brock would retrieve them.

Wait. Idiot! I turned on the siren. Traffic started peeling over to the shoulder and I continued my desperate race home.

The house was dark. The only sound was Shutterbug's frantic barking and the yelping of Sassy. Where was Morgan and my grandmother?

"Ruthie!" I opened my bedroom door to allow the dogs out. "Find your mama, Sassy. Find Ruthie."

The puppy's ears rose. Not even Shutterbug could be convinced to move. Ruthie wasn't in the house.

"Hello?" I darted from room to room, coming across Morgan standing on a stool in the shower, his hands restrained behind him, his tightly bound neck shackled to the shower head. Relief poured from him when I arrived. I pulled the duct tape from his mouth. "Where did Doug take Ruthie?"

"I don't know. Get me down from here without making me hang myself and we'll find out."

I opened a bathroom drawer and pulled out a

pair of scissors Ruthie used to trim her hair. I cut the silk scarf tied around Morgan's neck. "How in the world did Doug overpower you?"

"He hit me over the head while I was, uh, using the bathroom. Even bodyguards have to take care of business once in a while. The rat waited for his opportunity" He rubbed his wrists. "Put a leash on your dog and let's go find him." From the look on Morgan's face, Doug might not live long after we found him.

"Where are we going?" I hurried after him as he marched down the hall.

"I overheard him say something about the studio."

"I found the shoes and proof that Sawyer was in cahoots."

Morgan's steps faltered. "Where is he now?"

"I think he might be dead." I put a hand on Morgan to slow him down. "He shot Lori."

He jerked. "Is she alive?"

"She was when I left. She fired back. I don't know her condition. Brock stayed with her. Morgan, Doug had plans to marry my grandmother than hire Sawyer to kill her."

"And now those plans are kaput." He set his jaw. "Let's go."

Fear ripped through me like a knife through butter, cutting clear to my core. "He doesn't need her anymore."

"Except as a hostage."

He rushed to his room and withdrew a Glock from the bottom drawer of his nightstand. After checking for bullets, he strode to the front door, scooping up Sassy as he went. "I know I can't make you stay here, so please stay behind me at all times."

"You love Ruthie, don't you?"

He gave a wry smile. "I've loved her since the first time she danced for me. What a woman."

"Why didn't you go after her?" I asked, jumping into the passenger seat of the squad car.

"By the time I got up the nerve to ask the most beautiful woman in the world to go out with me, she'd stopped dancing and was dating your grandfather." He started the car and glanced at me. "I plan on changing that once she's safe."

"You save her, and I give you my blessing." I clicked my seatbelt into place and we raced for the studio.

I didn't think I'd ever prayed so hard in my life. Not even when it had been my life at stake. This time, the only family I had left was in danger, and I could hardly breathe.

Morgan reached over and squeezed my hand. "We'll get her."

I nodded, blinking back tears.

My cell phone rang. "Brock?"

"Yeah, it's me. What's happening?"

"Morgan and I are headed to the studio. We think that's where Doug has taken Ruthie."

"They were here."

"What?"

"Doug pulled up to the gate, saw the ambulance, then sped away. I'll meet you at the studio."

"We can't wait for you, Brock."

"I know."

"Lawrence?"

"Shot in the side. Still breathing when the paramedics loaded her into the ambulance. Sawyer is dead."

"Good," Morgan muttered. "Tell Mr. Handsome that if he's coming, he'd better hurry up and be prepared to fight."

CHAPTER TWENTY-FOUR

Brock's car was in the lot when we pulled in, but there was no sight of him. Parked next to the Jaguar was Ruthie's…my Corvette. The man not only wanted my grandmother but my vintage car as well. Not while I still breathed. I shoved my door open while Morgan called for backup and argued with the dispatcher as to why he had the squad car.

"Never mind that, woman! Send someone to help me." He threw down the radio and exited the car. "Some people have absolutely no sense."

With pepper spray in my hand and a gun in Morgan's, we entered the lot. Morgan held up his hand in the universal signal to stop. We listened for any sound that would tell us where they were.

"Where, Canyon?"

"I don't know. Doug's office, maybe. If not there, we can head to the shed where the files were stolen from." I hoped I was right. Every second we were delayed increased the risk to Ruthie.

I unclipped the leash from Shutterbug. "Find Ruthie."

Shutterbug, followed closely by the miniature Yorkie, headed in the direction of Doug's office. Morgan followed, with me staying closely behind him.

They might have been in the office at one time, but they were gone. Drawers hung open, proof that someone had wanted something very badly. So badly that they didn't close the drawers in their haste to leave, or they didn't find what they were looking for.

Shutterbug sniffed around for a few minutes, then darted from the building and raced across the lot. "She's headed for the storage shed," I said, speeding to catch up with her.

Loud voices came from the open doorway. I motioned for Shutterbug to stay and grabbed Sassy, putting my hand over her muzzle to keep her silent. The last thing we wanted was to tip Doug off that we were there. From Ruthie's shrill voice, she was unharmed and furious.

"I cannot believe you used me this way, Doug Lincoln. I liked you. I really did."

"I had no intention of you ever finding out," he replied. "I share your feelings, but I'm in dire straits."

"I don't care."

I strained my ears listening for Brock. Worry grew when I couldn't hear him. I needed to see inside.

Morgan stopped me. "Is there another way in?" he whispered.

"I don't think so. Unless it's blocked by boxes."

He motioned for me to follow him around to the back. A boarded-up window sat high on the wall. There was no way in except through the front door.

"Leave him alone!" Ruthie's voice reached us as we rounded the corner again. "You cannot harm Hollywood's Golden Boy, or every fan in America will be hunting you."

Doug laughed. "I doubt that. Someone new will come up and replace him within a month."

My eyes widened, and I glanced up at Morgan.

With a grim set to his mouth, he slid into the building, gun held at the ready. I followed, peering around him to locate Ruthie and Brock. Doug must have them in the back of the building. We eased toward their voices.

"Did you kill Ben and Junior Johnson?" Ruthie asked.

"No."

"All right then, did you have a part in their deaths?"

"Yes. Come now, dear, don't ask questions. The least you know the better. We can still get married and move to Europe—Italy, Spain, wherever you want. With your money we can live as royalty."

Ruthie's laugh lacked humor. "Why do you think I went back to acting, Doug? My money was running out. Buying your ex-wife's house took almost all of what I had left."

"That is unfortunate."

"You no longer have any use for me. That tells me your words of love were nothing more than lies." Her voice broke.

My heart ached for her. I couldn't take it anymore. With the pepper spray aimed in Doug's direction, I darted around Morgan and pressed the trigger.

A mere breath later, my eyes were streaming, and I was struggling to breathe. The good thing about my suffering was the fact that I'd inadvertently created a diversion for Morgan to step forward and disarm Doug, twisting his arms behind him.

"Grandma?" I tore off the belt that held her to the chair. "Are you all right?"

"Very much so, sweetheart, although my pride is wounded and my heart aches a bit."

I glanced from her to Morgan. "I think you'll be better soon enough. Where's Brock?"

"Doug hit him over the head and dragged him behind those boxes." She bent down and picked up an ecstatic Sassy. "My little darling would have protected me if she'd been able to."

"Watch him, Shutterbug."

My wonderful girl stationed herself next to Morgan and Doug, her dark eyes fixed on the man who cursed and twisted in the larger one's grasp.

I ducked behind a stack of files, relieved to see Brock stirring. I blinked through my streaming eyes and released him from his bindings.

"Your face is all red," he said.

"Pepper spray." I smiled. "You must be feeling better if you can comment on how bad a girl looks."

"You're the most beautiful thing I've ever seen." He sat up. "Where's Doug? How's Ruthie?"

"Morgan has them both."

"Look out!" Ruthie screamed.

Morgan cursed.

Shutterbug barked.

Seconds later, the door to the shed slammed closed and a lock clicked into place. My heart seized. "He'll set the building on fire like someone did the drug house."

Morgan held a hand to his bleeding side. "He had a knife. He bit me and pulled it from his pocket, the pig sticker."

"You or the knife?" Ruthie asked.

"The knife!" He glanced at the small window.

"Hanson, help me get these boards off. If he sets fire, it won't take long to burn."

"Wait. Where's my dog?" I glanced around the building.

"She must have gotten out," Brock said, tossing boxes aside in order to get to the window.

The first tendrils of smoke drifted under the door. Shutterbug barked. Doug screamed. Sirens wailed in the distance.

I had faith that my furry friend would keep Doug in check until the police arrived, but I wasn't sure it would be in time to save us. "What is with that man and fires?"

"You two might want to move faster," Ruthie said. "The front of the building is on fire."

I glanced over my shoulder to see flames licking the front door. "Hurry."

Brock and Morgan tossed boards to the floor finally clearing the building. "Come on ladies," Morgan held out his hand. "Ruthie?"

He helped her up, handing Sassy to her once she

was out. "Your turn, Kelly."

"You men won't fit." I coughed against the increasing smoke. "I won't go without you."

Brock put his hands on my shoulders. "Sweetheart, you have to. If you don't get out and stop that fire, we'll die in here."

Tears that had nothing to do with the pepper spray or smoke filled my eyes. "What if I can't?"

"We won't know that until you try." He lifted me in his arms and helped push me out the window.

I tried to remember where I'd seen a fire extinguisher. The cafeteria. Seeing that Shutterbug had Doug on the ground and stood guard over him and that his knife lay a few feet away, I darted for the larger building on my left.

"Halt."

I glanced over my shoulder to see two police officers racing toward me. "I need to stop the fire." I ducked into the cafeteria, surprised to see Rod nursing a cup of coffee. "Do you not know what's happening outside?"

"The noise?" He shrugged. "I thought they were filming."

"No, the storage shed is on fire and people are trapped in there." I yanked at the extinguisher on the wall.

"Oh." He took it from me and sprinted outside.

The cops had Doug handcuffed and off to the side while two of them tried breaking the burning front door down with metal chairs from the outside sitting area. Spotting us, one of them took the extinguisher from Rod and sprayed the door.

"We just need it calm enough to get them out."

Another officer headed to the back with an axe in his hand.

"Move." Rod pushed the officer away. Wearing gardening gloves he pulled from his pocket, he inserted a key into the padlock and kicked the door open. Then, he stepped back, and beat at the flickers of fire trying to burn through his coveralls.

Morgan and Brock staggered out, drawing in great gulps of air and collapsing to the pavement. I sat next to Brock and put one arm around him and the other around Shutterbug. "We did it," I said. "Found justice for another Hollywood murder."

"And you found fodder for another book," Ruthie said, sitting next to us. "I never thought researching for a book would be this dangerous."

I released Shutterbug and took her hand. "Are you okay?"

She nodded. "I'm fine. I always knew there was something off about Doug, but I was feeling a little lonely with you working all the time and thought maybe a man might fill the void."

"His name is actually Donald Lakin, and he has a huge gambling problem."

"Huh." She frowned. "That's why he always forgot his wallet when we ate out and I'd end up paying. Drat. Now, I have to find a new agent. Do you know how hard that is?"

"Not really." I grinned. "But I doubt it will be too hard since we're not out-of-work actors. Just make sure that our new one doesn't gamble away their share of the royalties and have to resort to crime to pay their bills."

"I think I'll go with a woman this time. We're

much more sensible.”

We laughed and climbed to our feet. It had been a long day and the men still needed to be treated for smoke inhalation, as stated several times by the waiting paramedics. While the paramedics took care of the men, Ruthie and I sat at the outdoor eating area and waited.

“Morgan cares for you,” I said.

“He does?” Her eyes widened.

“He’s a good man.”

“And not involved in show biz. That’s a major bonus. I don’t have much luck with Hollywood men, even the short pudgy ones. I suppose you found all the evidence you need to put Doug away?”

“Yes, and Sawyer, who actually did the killing, is dead. This case is closed.”

She breathed deeply through her nose, releasing it slowly out her mouth. “Now, Lawrence can focus on solving Kevin’s murder.”

“Yes.” Shutterbug and I intended to help in any way we could.

The End

Dear Reader,

I hope you're having as much fun with my new series as I am. Isn't Ruthie a hoot and Brock Handsome, uh, Hanson is as pretty inside as out. I love writing about feisty heroines and Kelly is no exception. Maybe one of these days, she'll actually find out what career to settle on, but until then, we'll tag along for another wild ride in the upcoming book three, Shoot to Kill.

Reviews are very important to authors. If you enjoyed Killer Snapshot, I'd be blessed if you left a review and signed up for my newsletter http://cynthiahickey.com/sign-up-for-my-newsletter-to-keep-uptodate-on-news-and-new-releases/

We've always got something going on over there. You never know. You might win a prize.

If you missed book one, you can get it here Killer Pose, book 1

Of Shoot to Kill, book 3. Get it here

God bless,

Cynthia Hickey

Keep reading for the first chapter of Shoot to Kill

CHAPTER ONE

I was dead. Deceased. About to be buried. I, Kelly Canyon, wannabe crime reporter, current actor and photographer, stared at the brand-spanking new, hot-red Jimmy Choos hanging from my dog's mouth. Grandma, or Ruthie, as she preferred to be called, was going to kill me and Shutterbug. "Drop it, girl." What was with my normally well-trained dog and shoes?

Ruthie marched into the room, set her Yorkie, Sassy, on the sofa and pointed at Shutterbug. "Drop them this instant."

The shoes fell to the floor with a thud. Shutterbug's ears perked-up and she tilted her head to the side, looking very pleased with herself.

"I'm sorry, Ruthie." I grinned sheepishly. "We were just about to head out the door to scope out the venue for the award's ceremony when she trotted out of your room with these."

"The very shoes I plan on wearing to receive my award." Ruthie snatched the shoes from the floor and flipped them over in her hands. "Nothing but drool." She wagged a finger at Shutterbug. "You are one lucky dog." With her nose in the air, Ruthie whirled and marched to her room.

"At least we're still breathing." I snapped my fingers for my furry best friend to follow me outside. Since it was just the two of us, I buckled her into the passenger seat of my 1965 candy apple red Corvette. Soon, we were zooming toward Hollywood Boulevard.

Ruthie was going to receive a lifetime achievement award. With our most recent season of our mother/daughter cop drama, her fame had grown. Well, mine too, but I much preferred the attention I received from writing a book based on each of the last two murders I'd help solve. Book number one stayed on the best-seller list and I had high hopes for book two. Soon, I wouldn't have to act and could devote all my time to photography and writing.

Yes, I'd given up on becoming a crime reporter. I got paid more from being an author and still took photographs for fun and a little pocket money, as Ruthie called it.

I'd volunteered to take photos at the award ceremony where Ruthie would receive the award. Brock was emceeing the event and would be more handsome than was legal. I still couldn't believe he called me his girlfriend.

I parked behind the theater and let Shutterbug out of the car. She dashed ahead of me, stopping at the door with an excited yip. I smiled, spotting Brock's car. He'd arrived first and probably had Brutus with him. Good. The dogs could play while we worked.

Brutus, an English Mastiff around six months old would catch up in size to Shutterbug very soon. The gangly pup barreled toward us. The only thing that kept me from being bowled over was Shutterbug leaping between us to play.

"Good morning." Brock strolled my way, a smile highlighting his handsome features.

"Good morning." I lifted my face for his kiss. "Been scoping out the best places for your promo pics?"

He obliged with the kiss. "I think I've found a few places that will work. Let's see what your expert eyes say." He slid his arm around my waist.

A few minutes later, we entered a dressing room. "I thought maybe one of me in front of the mirror for makeup. Then another of me in my tux and maybe a few candid pictures of me on stage just hanging around in my jeans and tee shirt."

I nodded. The candid ones would be the best. Brock looked very good in jeans and a tee shirt. "Maybe a couple of you and Brutus?"

"If we can get him to sit still long enough. He's got enough energy for three dogs."

"Shutterbug got Ruthie's shoes again." I sagged onto a chaise lounge. "I might have to get my own place."

He sat next to me. "Not in a million years. Ruthie would never kick you or Shutterbug out. Despite her grumbles, she loves your dog almost as much as that yappy thing she takes everywhere with her."

A few months back, I'd bought Ruthie the Yorkie pup to ease her loneliness when I wasn't around. Brock had found Brutus around the same time, and life became pretty chaotic with three dogs under one year in age. I wouldn't trade a minute of it. Then, to spite the local law enforcement who often accused me of interfering, all three of us had our pups certified as service dogs so they could go with us everywhere. Shutterbug had proven her worth already by taking down a criminal.

"Let's get started," I said, "I need to read over my script for next season. We start filming on Monday." Today was Friday and the ceremony tonight, but weekends often got away from me. Not entirely true. The beach called to me way too often on the weekends for me to get any reading done.

Brock led the way to the stage and whistled for Brutus. The pup lumbered down the aisle and bounded onto the stage.

I took a few shots of Brock and the pup wrestling, then some posed ones of them on the stage steps, before taking a few of Brock alone. Not an easy thing to do with a large puppy that wanted to photobomb the shoot.

The ones of Brock having his makeup done and wearing his tux would have to wait until after the ceremony that night. He wore makeup now, but fans liked to see the process of getting Hollywood glam, so we'd pretend. I packed up my camera and studied the room. Plush red chairs faced the stage. A matching carpet runner ran down the aisle, promising that everyone who entered would receive the royal treatment. The venue wasn't as large as the one that housed the Oscars, but still impressive with two thousand seats and a balcony that held a thousand more.

"Is Leo's catering?" I glanced at Brock.

"Yep. Let's hope the night doesn't end with a crab leg in someone's neck." He shuddered.

"Don't remind me." I'd thought the death of

Lauren Matthews to have been my first experience with murder, but I couldn't have been more wrong. It was my second. My father's death was the first, as it turned out. Then the maintenance man, Bob, was the third. A movie studio or random traffic stop couldn't prevent evil doings.

Later that evening, I hung back as Brock escorted Ruthie up the red carpet. I wasn't his date this time. Just like a year ago, I was a member of those photographers, hungrily snapping pix of the arriving celebrities. The only change…I could focus this time on Brock and Ruthie and didn't have to rely on selling the photos to pay my bills. Also, like a year ago, I had a special pass to get into the theater and go anywhere I pleased.

Which I did. I slipped away from the crowd the moment Brock and Ruthie stepped into the theater and made my way around to the back door. After flashing my ID badge to the muscled guard, I entered the building and headed for Brock's room. He would be the only star receiving makeup. Everyone else would take their seats immediately.

"Hey, Lisa." I greeted the artist who did Ruthie's and my makeup for our show. "I'm glad they let you do Brock."

"Me, too." She held out a trembling hand. "I've never worked on someone so gorgeous before. What if I mess up?"

"Don't think of him as Mr. Handsome." I plopped on the lounge. "Think of him as a pesky neighbor kid with an annoying dog."

"I heard that." Brock entered and came straight to me for a kiss before flashing Lisa a grin. "I don't bite."

Instead of calming her, his smile made her more nervous. "I know," she said softly. "Good grief. I can hack into computers, erase dark shadows under a person's eyes, so I think I can do a simple makeup job."

"Good. If my agent hadn't insisted I look my best under the harsh lights, I'd skip this part." He sat in the chair and raised his chin so she could put an apron around his neck.

I snapped a few photos, then sat back and enjoyed feasting my eyes on a man as gorgeous inside as out. No wonder fans called him Hollywood's Golden Boy. Not because of his looks, not because of his almost black hair and sky-blue eyes, but because of his kindness.

He caught me feasting and gave me that tender smile he reserved for me. The one that sent my heart into flips.

"Ready?" I stood and handed him the tuxedo hanging on a rod. "I'll wait outside and walk with you to the stage."

"Great." He glanced in the mirror. "You did a super job, Lisa. The lights won't wash me out."

Her eyes widened. "Does that mean I went too dark?"

He chuckled. "You did just right."

She exhaled heavily. "Great. It'll look good on my resume to add your name." She flashed a grin, then hurried from the room.

"You look like you have a tan," I whispered on my way out the door.

His laugh followed. True to form, Brock hadn't wanted to hurt her feelings. While he possessed enough ego to fit into Hollywood, he was also humble enough not to hurt someone's feelings. God broke the mold when he made Brock Hanson.

I reached over and toggled the light switch on the hall to get some good lighting when Brock exited his room. The hall remained dim, lit by a single light in the direction of the stage.

This wouldn't work at all. I flagged down a man in dark blue coveralls. "This light isn't working."

"So?" He pulled the brim of his cap down lower over his eyes.

"It's too dark. I can't see you, and you're only an arm's length away. How am I supposed to take pictures?"

"Fine. Follow me." He led me in the opposite direction to a dead end. We turned and headed down another hall.

"Do you know where we're going?"

"No, I'm new. I'm looking for the fuse box and got turned around. There it is." He opened a green metal box on the wall and flipped a couple of switches.

The hall behind us blazed to life. "That's bright enough to land a plane. Will that work?"

"Yes."

He rushed away, leaving me alone. The dude might be maintenance, at least that's what he looked like, but the man was plain rude.

I slammed the door to the fuse box and turned to

leave. Brock would be ready to go, and we were cutting it close to showtime.

Something caught my attention from the corner of my eye. I turned and glanced behind a large cement post used to support the floor above. A man sat against the concrete block wall. A knife protruded from his white tee shirt-covered chest, and blood ran into the waistband of his green plaid boxer shorts.

Read the rest by scanning this code

www.cynthiahickey.com

Cynthia Hickey is a multi-published and best-selling author of cozy mysteries and romantic suspense. She has taught writing at many conferences and small writing retreats. She and her husband run the publishing press, Winged Publications. They live in Arizona and Arkansas, becoming snowbirds with three dogs. They have ten grandchildren who keep them busy and tell everyone they know that "Nana is a writer."

Connect with me on FaceBook
Twitter
Sign up for my newsletter and receive a free short story
www.cynthiahickey.com

Follow me on Amazon
And Bookbub
Shop my bookstore on shopify. For better price and autographed.

Enjoy other books by Cynthia Hickey

Misty Hollow
Secrets of Misty Hollow

Deceptive Peace
Calm Surface
Lightning Never Strikes Twice
Lethal Inheritance
Bitter Isolation
Say I Don't
Christmas Stalker
Bridge to Safety

Stay in Misty Hollow for a while. Get the entire series here!

The Seven Deadly Sins series
Deadly Pride
Deadly Covet
Deadly Lust
Deadly Glutton
Deadly Envy
Deadly Sloth
Deadly Anger

The Tail Waggin' Mysteries
Cat-Eyed Witness
The Dog Who Found a Body
Troublesome Twosome
Four-Legged Suspect
Unwanted Christmas Guest
Wedding Day Cat Burglar

Brothers Steele

Sharp as Steele
Carved in Steele
Forged in Steele
Brothers Steele (All three in one)

The Brothers of Copper Pass
Wyatt's Warrant
Dirk's Defense
Stetson's Secret
Houston's Hope
Dallas's Dare
Seth's Sacrifice
Malcolm's Misunderstanding
The Brothers of Copper Pass Boxed Set

Time Travel
The Portal

Tiny House Mysteries
No Small Caper
Caper Goes Missing
Caper Finds a Clue
Caper's Dark Adventure
A Strange Game for Caper
Caper Steals Christmas
Caper Finds a Treasure
Tiny House Mysteries boxed set

Wife for Hire – Private Investigators

Saving Sarah
Lesson for Lacey
Mission for Meghan
Long Way for Lainie
Aimed at Amy
Wife for Hire (all five in one)

A Hollywood Murder
Killer Pose, book 1
Killer Snapshot, book 2
Shoot to Kill, book 3
Kodak Kill Shot, book 4
To Snap a Killer
Hollywood Murder Mysteries

Shady Acres Mysteries
Beware the Orchids, book 1
Path to Nowhere
Poison Foliage
Poinsettia Madness
Deadly Greenhouse Gases
Vine Entrapment
Shady Acres Boxed Set

CLEAN BUT GRITTY Romantic Suspense

Highland Springs

Murder Live
Say Bye to Mommy

To Breathe Again
Highland Springs Murders (all 3 in one)

Colors of Evil Series

Shades of Crimson
Coral Shadows

The Pretty Must Die Series

Ripped in Red, book 1
Pierced in Pink, book 2
Wounded in White, book 3
Worthy, The Complete Story

Lisa Paxton Mystery Series

Eenie Meenie Miny Mo
Jack Be Nimble
Hickory Dickory Dock
Boxed Set

Hearts of Courage

A Heart of Valor
The Game
Suspicious Minds
After the Storm
Local Betrayal
Hearts of Courage Boxed Set

Overcoming Evil series
Mistaken Assassin
Captured Innocence
Mountain of Fear
Exposure at Sea
A Secret to Die for
Collision Course
Romantic Suspense of 5 books in 1

INSPIRATIONAL

Nosy Neighbor Series
Anything For A Mystery, **Book 1**
A Killer Plot, **Book 2**
Skin Care Can Be Murder, **Book 3**
Death By Baking, **Book 4**
Jogging Is Bad For Your Health, **Book 5**
Poison Bubbles, **Book 6**
A Good Party Can Kill You, **Book 7**
Nosy Neighbor collection

Christmas with Stormi Nelson

The Summer Meadows Series
Fudge-Laced Felonies, **Book 1**
Candy-Coated Secrets, **Book 2**
Chocolate-Covered Crime, **Book 3**
Maui Macadamia Madness, **Book 4**
All four novels in one collection

The River Valley Mystery Series
Deadly Neighbors, **Book 1**
Advance Notice, **Book 2**
The Librarian's Last Chapter, **Book 3**
All three novels in one collection

Contemporary

Romance in Paradise
Maui Magic
Sunset Kisses
Deep Sea Love
3 in 1

Finding a Way Home
Service of Love
Hillbilly Cinderella
Unraveling Love
I'd Rather Kiss My Horse

Christmas
Dear Jillian
Romancing the Fabulous Cooper Brothers
Handcarved Christmas
The Payback Bride
Curtain Calls and Christmas Wishes
Christmas Gold
A Christmas Stamp

Snowflake Kisses
Merry's Secret Santa
A Christmas Deception

The Red Hat's Club (Contemporary novellas)

Finally
Suddenly
Surprisingly
The **Red Hat's Club 3 – in 1**

Short Story

One Hour (A short story thriller)
Whisper Sweet Nothings (a Valentine short romance)